Peggy Moseley.

1020 Riverside

Evansville

Ind—

THE LITTLE COLONEL'S

(Trade Mark)

HERO

THE LITTLE COLONEL AND HER HERO

The Little Colonel's Hero

By ANNIE FELLOWS JOHNSTON

Author of " The Little Colonel," " Two Little Knights
of Kentucky," " Big Brother," " Asa Holmes," "The
Little Colonel's House Party," " The Little Colonel's
Holidays," etc.

Music by ALBION FELLOWS BACON

Illustrated by ETHELDRED B. BARRY

BOSTON ❋ THE PAGE
COMPANY ❋ PUBLISHERS

Twenty-first Impression, April, 1919
Twenty-second Impression, October, 1919

CONTENTS

LIST OF ILLUSTRATIONS

———◆———

THE LITTLE COLONEL'S HERO

(Trade Mark)

───────

CHAPTER I.

HER TWELFTH BIRTHDAY

"OH, Tarbaby! *Everybody* has forgotten that it is my birthday! Even Papa Jack has gone off to town without saying a word about it, and he nevah did such a thing befo' in all his life!"

As she spoke, the Little Colonel put her arm around her pony's neck, and for a moment her fair little head was pressed disconsolately against its velvety black mane.

"It isn't the presents I care about," she whispered, choking back a heart-broken sob; "but oh, Tarbaby, it's the bein' forgotten! Of co'se mothah couldn't be expected to remembah, she's been so ill. But I think grandfathah might, or Mom Beck, or *somebody*. If there'd only been one single person when I came down-stairs this mawnin' to say 'I wish you many happy returns, Lloyd, deah,' I wouldn't feel so bad. But there wasn't, and I nevah felt so misah'ble and lonesome and left out since I was bawn."

Tarbaby had no words with which to comfort his little mistress, but he seemed to understand that she was in trouble, and rubbed his nose lovingly against her shoulder. The mute caress comforted her as much as words could have done, and presently she climbed into the saddle and started slowly down the avenue to the gate.

It was a warm May morning, sweet with the fragance of the locusts, for the great trees arching above her were all abloom, and the ground beneath was snowy with the wind-blown petals. Under the long white arch she rode, with the fallen blossoms white at her feet. The pewees called from the cedars and the fat red-breasted robins ran across the lawn just as they had done the spring before, when it was her eleventh birthday, and she had ridden along that same way singing, the happiest hearted child in the Valley. But she was not singing to-day. Another sob came up in her throat as she thought of the difference.

" Now I'm a whole yeah oldah," she sighed. " Oh, deah ! I don't want to grow up, one bit, and I'll be suah 'nuff old on my next birthday, for I'll be in my teens then. I wondah how that will feel. This last yeah was such a lovely one, for it brought the house pahty and so many holidays. But this yeah has begun all wrong. I can't help feelin' that it's goin' to bring me lots of trouble."

Half-way down the avenue she thought she heard some one calling her, and stopped to look back. But no one was in sight. The shutters were closed in her mother's room.

"Last yeah she stood at the window and waved to me when I rode away," sighed the child, her eyes filling with tears again. "Now she's so white and ill it makes me cry to look at her. Maybe that is the trouble this yeah is goin' to bring me. Betty's mothah died, and Eugenia's, and maybe" — but the thought was too dreadful to put into words, and she stopped abruptly.

"Mom Beck was right," she whispered with a nod of her head. "She said that sad thoughts are like crows. They come in flocks. I wish I could stop thinkin' about such mou'nful things."

A train passed as she cantered through the gate and started down the road beside the railroad track. She drew rein to watch it thunder by. Some child at the window pointed a finger at her, and then two smiling little faces were pressed against the pane for an eager glimpse. It was the prettiest wayside picture the passengers had seen in all that morning's travel — the Little Colonel on her pony, with the spray of locust bloom in the cockade of the Napoleon cap she wore, and a plume of the same graceful blossoms nodding jauntily over each of Tarbaby's black ears.

As the admiring faces whirled past her, Lloyd drew a long breath of relief. "I'm glad that I don't have to do my riding in a smoky old car this May mawnin'," she thought. "It is wicked for me to be so unhappy when I have Tarbaby and all the othah things that mothah and Papa Jack have given me. I know perfectly well that they love me just the same even if they have forgotten my birthday, and I won't let such old black crow thoughts flock down on me. I'll ride fast and get away from them."

That was harder to do than she had imagined, for as she passed Judge Moore's place the deserted house added to her feeling of loneliness. Andy, the old gardener, was cutting the grass on the front lawn. She called to him.

"When is the family coming out from town, Andy?"

"Not this summer, Miss Lloyd," he answered. "It'll be the first summer in twenty years that the

Judge has missed. He has taken a cottage at the seaside, and they're all going there. The house will stay closed, just as you see it now, I reckon, for another year."

"At the seashore!" she echoed. "Not coming out!" She almost gasped, the news was so unexpected. Here was another disappointment, and a very sore one. Every summer, as far back as she could remember, Rob Moore had been her favourite playfellow. Now there would be no more mad Tam O'Shanter races, with Rob clattering along beside her on his big iron-gray horse. No more good times with the best and jolliest of little neighbours. A summer without Rob's cheery whistle and good-natured laugh would seem as empty and queer as the woods without the bird voices, or the meadows without the whirr of humming things. She rode slowly on.

There was no letter for her when she stopped at the post-office to inquire for the mail. The girls on whom she called afterward were not at home, so she rode aimlessly around the Valley until nearly lunch-time, wishing for once that it were a school-day. It was the longest Saturday morning she had ever known. She could not practise her music lesson for fear of making her mother's headache worse. She could not go near the kitchen, where she might have found entertainment, for Aunt Cindy was in one of her black tempers, and scolded shrilly as she moved around among her shining tins.

There was no one to show her how to begin her new piece of embroidery ; Papa Jack had forgotten to bring out the magazines she wanted to see ; Walker had failed to roll the tennis-court and put up the net, so she could not even practise serving the balls by herself.

When lunch-time came, it was so lonely eating by herself in the big dining-room, that she hurried through the meal as quickly as possible, and tiptoed up the stairs to the door of her mother's room. Mom Beck raised her finger with a warning "Sh!" and seeing that her mother was still asleep, Lloyd stole away to her own room, her own pretty pink and white nest, and curled herself up among the cushions in a big easy chair by the window.

It was the first time in her memory that her mother had been ill. For more than a week she had not been able to leave her room, and the lonely child, accustomed to being with her constantly, crept around the house like a little stray kitten. The place scarcely seemed like home, and the days were endless. Some unusual feeling of sensitiveness had

kept her from reminding the family of her birthday.
Other years she had openly counted the days, for
weeks beforehand, and announced the gifts that she
would be most pleased to receive.

Here by the window the dismal crow thoughts
began flocking down to her again, and to drive them
away she picked up a book from the table and began
to read. It was a green and gold volume of short
stories, one that she had read many times before, but
she never grew tired of them.

The one she liked best was " Marguerite's Wonder-
ball," and she turned to that first, because it was the
story of a happy birthday. Marguerite was a little
German girl, learning to knit, and to help her in her
task her family wound for her a mammoth ball of
yarn, as full of surprise packages as a plum cake
is of plums. Day by day, as her patient knitting
unwound the yarn, some gift dropped out into her
lap. They were simple things, nearly all of them.
A knife, a ribbon, a thimble, a pencil, and here and
there a bonbon, but they were magnified by the
charm of the surprise, and they turned the tedious
task into a pleasant pastime. Not until her birthday
was the knitting finished, and as she took the last
stitches a little velvet-covered jewel-box fell out. In
the jewel-box was a string of pearls that had belonged

to Marguerite's great-great-grandmother. It was a precious family heirloom, and although Marguerite could not wear the necklace until she was old enough to go to her first great court ball, it made her very proud and happy to think that, of all the grandchildren in the family, she had been chosen as the one to wear her great-great-grandmother's name that means pearl, and had inherited on that account the beautiful Von Behren necklace.

When the knitting was done there was a charming birthday feast in her honour. They crowned her with flowers, and every one, even the dignified old grandfather, did her bidding until nightfall, because it was *her* day, and she was its queen.

Closing the book Lloyd lay back among the cushions, smiling for the twentieth time over Marguerite's happiness, and planning the beautiful wonder-ball she herself would like to have, if wonder-balls were to be had for the wishing. It should be as big as a cart-wheel, and the first gift to be unwound should be a tiny ring set with an emerald, because that is the lucky stone for people born in May. She already owned so many books, and trinkets, that she hardly knew what else to wish for unless it might be a coral fan chain and a mother-of-pearl manicure set. But deep down in the heart of the ball she would like to find a wishing-

"CLOSING THE BOOK LLOYD LAY BACK AMONG THE
CUSHIONS"

nut, that would grant her wishes like an Aladdin's lamp whenever it was rubbed.

She must have fallen asleep in the midst of her day-dreaming, for it seemed to her that it was only a minute after she closed her book, that she heard the half-past five o'clock train whistling at the station, and while she was still rubbing her eyes she saw her father coming up the avenue.

All day she had had a lingering hope that he might bring her something when he came out from the city. " If it's nothing but a bag of peanuts," she thought, "it will be better than having a birthday go by without anything, 'specially when all the othahs have been neahly as nice as Christmas."

She peeped out between the curtains, scanning him eagerly as he came toward the house, but there was no package in either hand, and no suggestive parcel bulged from any of his pockets.

" I'll not be a baby," Lloyd whispered to herself, winking her eyelids rapidly to clear away a sort of mist that seemed to blur the landscape. " I'm too old to care so much."

Still, it was such a disappointment, added to all the others that the day had brought, that she buried her face in the cushions and cried softly. She could hear her father's voice in the next room, presently.

It seemed quite loud and cheerful; more cheerful than it had sounded since her mother's dreadful neuralgic headaches had begun. A few minutes later she heard her mother laugh. It was such a welcome sound, that she hastily dried her eyes and started to run in to see what had caused it, but she paused as she passed the mirror. Her eyes were so red that she knew she would be questioned, and she concluded it would be better to wait until she was dressed for dinner.

So she sat looking out of the window till the big hall clock struck six, and then hastily bathing her eyes, she slipped into a fresh white dress, and looking carefully at herself in the mirror, concluded that she had waited long enough. To her surprise, she found her mother sitting up in a big Morris chair by the window. Maybe it was the pink silk kimono she wore that brought a faint tinge of colour to her cheeks, but whatever it was, she looked well and natural again, and for the first time in six long days the neuralgic headache was all gone, and the lines of suffering were smoothed out of her face.

The wide glass doors opening on to the balcony were standing open, and through the vines stole the golden sunset light, the chirping of robins, the smell of new-mown grass, and the heavy sweetness of the locust blooms. Lloyd rubbed her eyes, thinking she surely must be dreaming. There on the vine-covered balcony stood a table all set as if for a "pink party." There were flowers and bonbons in the silver dishes, and in the centre Mom Beck was proudly placing a mammoth birthday cake, wreathed in pink icing roses, and crowned with twelve pink candles ready for the lighting.

"Oh, mothah!" she cried. "I — I thought — "

She did not finish the sentence, but something in her surprised tone, the sudden flushing of her face, and the traces of tears still in her eyes, told what she meant.

"You thought mother had forgotten," whispered Mrs. Sherman, tenderly, as Lloyd hid her face on her shoulder.

"No, not for one minute, dear. But the pain was so bad this morning, when you came to my room, that I couldn't talk. Then you were out riding so long this morning, and when I wakened after lunch and sent Mom Beck to find you, she said you were asleep in your room. Papa Jack and I have been planning a great surprise for you, and he did not want to mention it until all the arrangements were completed. That is why there was no birthday surprise for you at breakfast. But you'll soon be a very happy little girl, for this surprise is something you have been wanting for more than a year."

How suddenly the whole world had changed for the Little Colonel! The sunshine had never seemed so golden, the locust blooms so deliciously sweet. Her birthday had not been forgotten, after all. Mrs. Sherman's chair was wheeled to the table on the balcony, and Lloyd took her seat with sparkling eyes. She wondered what the surprise could be, and felt sure that Papa Jack would not tell her until the cake was cut, and the last birthday wish made with the blowing of the birthday candles.

He had intended to save his news to serve with the dessert, but when he questioned Lloyd as to how she had spent the day, and laughed at her for reading the old tale of Marguerite's wonder-ball so many times, his secret escaped him before he knew it. Turning to Mrs. Sherman he said, "By the way, Elizabeth, our birthday gift for Lloyd might be called a sort of wonder-ball." Then he looked at his little daughter with a teasing smile, as he continued, "I wonder if you can guess my riddle. At first your wonder-ball will unroll a day and night on the cars, then a drive through a park where you rode in a baby-carriage once upon a time, but through which you shall go in an automobile this time, if you wish.

There'll be some shopping, maybe, and after that flags flying, and bands playing, and crowds of people waving good-bye."

He had intended to stop there, but the wondering expression on her face carried him on further. "I can't undertake to say how much your wonder-ball can hold, but somewhere near the centre of it will be a meeting with Betty and Eugenia, and perhaps a glimpse of the Gate of the Giant Scissors that you are always talking about."

As Lloyd listened a look of utter astonishment crept over her face. Then she suddenly sprang from her chair, and running to her father put a hand on each shoulder. "Papa Jack," she cried, breathlessly, "look me straight in the eyes! Are you in earnest? You don't mean that we are going abroad, do you? It *couldn't* be anything so lovely as that, could it?"

For answer he drew an envelope from his pocket and shook it before her eyes. "Look for yourself," he said. "This is to show that we are listed for passage on a steamer going to Antwerp the first of June. You may begin to pack your trunk next week, if you wish."

It was impossible for Lloyd to eat any more after that. She was too excited and happy, and there were countless questions she wanted to ask. "It's bettah than a hundred house pahties," she exclaimed, as she blew out the last birthday candle. "It's the loveliest wondah-ball that evah was, and I'm suah that nobody in all Kentucky is as happy as I am now."

CHAPTER II.

THE WONDER-BALL BEGINS TO UNWIND

LLOYD'S wonder-ball began to unroll the morning that her father took her to town to choose her own steamer trunk, and some of the things that were to go in it. She packed and unpacked it many times in the two weeks that followed, although she knew that Mom Beck would do the final packing, and probably take out half the things which she insisted upon crowding into it.

Every morning it was a fresh delight to waken and find it standing by her dressing-table, reminding her of the journey they would soon begin together, and, when the journey was actually begun, she settled back in her seat with a happy sigh.

"Now, I'll commence to count my packages as they fall out," she said. "I think I ought to count what I see from the car windows as one, for I enjoy looking out at the different places we pass moah than I evah enjoyed my biggest pictuah books."

"Then count this number two," said her father,

25

putting a flat, square parcel in her lap. Lloyd looked puzzled as she opened it. There was only a blank book inside, bound in Russia leather, with the word "Record" stamped on it in gilt.

"I thought it would be a good idea to keep a partnership diary," he said. "We can take turns in writing in it, and some day, when you are grown, and your mother and I are old and gray, it will help us to remember much of the journey that otherwise might pass out of our memories. So many things happen when one is travelling, that they are apt to crowd each other out of mind unless a record is kept of them."

"We'll begin as soon as we get on the ship," said Lloyd. "Mothah shall write first, then you, and then I. And let's put photographs in it, too, as Mrs. Walton did in hers. It will be like writing a real book. Package numbah two is lovely, Papa Jack."

It happened that Mr. Sherman was the only one who made an entry in the record for more than a week. Mrs. Sherman felt the motion of the vessel too much to be able to do more than lie out on deck in her steamer-chair. The Little Colonel, while she was not at all seasick, was afraid to attempt writing until she reached land.

"SOON SHE BEGAN WALKING UP AND DOWN THE DECK"

"The table jiggles so!" she complained, when she sat down at a desk in the ship's library. "I'm afraid that I'll spoil the page. You write it, Papa Jack." She put back the pen, and stood at his elbow while he wrote.

"Put down about all the steamah lettahs that we got," she suggested, "and the little Japanese stove Allison Walton sent me for my muff, and the books Rob sent. Oh, yes! And the captain's name and how long the ship is, and how many tons of things to eat they have on board. Mom Beck won't believe me when I tell her, unless I can show it to her in black and white."

After they had explored the vessel together, her father was ready to settle down in his deck-chair in a sheltered corner, and read aloud or sleep. But the Little Colonel grew tired of being wrapped like a mummy in her steamer rug. She did not care to read long at a time, and she grew tired of looking at nothing but water. Soon she began walking up and down the deck, looking for something to entertain her. In one place some little girls were busy with scissors and paint-boxes, making paper dolls. Farther along two boys were playing checkers, and, under the stairs, a group of children, gathered around their governess, were listening to a fairy tale. Lloyd longed to join them, for she fairly ached for some amusement. She paused an instant, with her hand on the rail, as she heard one sentence: "And the white prince, clasping the crystal ball, waved his plumed cap to the gnome, and vanished."

Wondering what the story was about, Lloyd walked around to the other side of the deck, only to find another long uninteresting row of sleepy figures stretched out in steamer-chairs, and half hidden in rugs and cloaks. She turned to go back, but paused as she caught sight of a girl, about her own age, standing against the deck railing, looking over into the sea. She was not a pretty girl. Her face was too dark and thin, according to Lloyd's standard of beauty, and her mouth looked as if it were used to saying disagreeable things.

But Lloyd thought her interesting, and admired the scarlet jacket she wore, with its gilt braid and buttons, and the scarlet cap that made her long plaits of hair look black as a crow's wing by contrast. Her hair was pretty, and hung far below her waist, tied at the end with two bows of scarlet ribbon.

The girl glanced up as Lloyd passed, and although there was a cool stare in her queer black eyes, Lloyd found herself greatly interested. She wanted to make the stranger's acquaintance, and passed back

and forth several times, to steal another side glance
at her. As she turned for the third time to retrace
her steps, she was nearly knocked off her feet by
two noisy boys, who bumped against her. They
were playing horse, to the annoyance of all the passengers on deck, stepping on people's toes, knocking
over chairs, and stumbling against the stewards who
were hurrying along with their heavy trays of beef
tea and lemonade.

Lloyd had seen the boys several times before.
They were little fellows of six and nine, with unusually thin legs and shrill voices, and were always eating.

Every time a deck steward passed, they grabbed a
share of whatever he carried. They seemed to have
discovered some secret passage to the ship's supplies.
Their blouses were pouched out all around with the
store of gingersnaps, nuts, and apples which they
had managed to stow away as a reserve fund. Lloyd
had seen the larger boy draw out six bananas, one
after another, from his blouse, and then squirm and
wriggle and almost stand on his head to reach the
seventh, which had slipped around to his back while
he was eating the others. They were munching
raisins now, as they ran.

After their collision with Lloyd they stopped running, and suddenly began calling, " Here, Fido !

Here, Fido!" Lloyd looked around eagerly, expecting to see some pet dog, and wishing that she had one of the many pet animals left behind at Locust, to amuse her now. But no dog was in sight. The girl in the scarlet jacket turned around with an angry scowl.

"Stop calling me that, Howl Sattawhite!" she exclaimed, crossly. "I'll tell mamma. You know what she said she'd do to you if you called me anything but Fidelia."

"And you know what she said she'd do to you if you kept calling me Howl," shouted the larger of the boys, making a saucy face and darting forward to give one of her long plaits of hair a sudden pull.

Quick as a flash, Fidelia turned, and catching him by the wrists, twisted them till he began to whimper with pain, and tried to set his teeth in her hand.

"You *dare* bite me, you little beast!" she cried. "You just dare, and I'll tell mamma how you spit at the waiter the morning we left the hotel."

Lloyd was scandalised. They were quarrelling like two little dogs, seemingly unconscious of the fact that a hundred people were within hearing. As Fidelia seemed to be getting the upper hand, the little brother joined in, calling in a high piping voice, "And if you squeal on Howell, Fidelia Sattawhite,

I'll tell mamma how you went out walking by yourself in New York when she told you not to, and took her new purse and lost it! So there, Miss Smarty!"

"Oh, those dreadful American children!" said an English woman near Lloyd. "They're all alike. At least the ones who travel. I have never seen any yet that had any manners. They are all pert and spoiled. Fancy an English child, now, making such a scene in public!"

The Little Colonel could feel her face growing painfully red. She was indignant at being classed with such rude children, and walked quickly away. At the cabin door she met a maid, who, coming out on deck with something wrapped carefully in an embroidered shawl, sat down on one of the empty benches.

Scarcely was she seated when the two boys pounced down upon her and began pulling at the blanket. "Oh, let me see Beauty, Fanchette," begged Howell. "Make him sit up and do some tricks."

The maid pushed them away with a strong hand, and then carefully drew aside a corner of the covering. Lloyd gave an exclamation of pleasure, for the head that popped out was that of a bright little French poodle. She had thought many times that morning of the two Bobs, and good old Fritz, dead and gone, of Boots, the hunting-dog, and the goat and the gobbler and the parrot, — all the animals she had loved and played with at Locust, wishing she had them with her. Now as she saw the bright eyes of the poodle peeping over the blanket, she forgot that she was a stranger, and running across the deck, she stooped down beside it.

"Oh, the darling little dog!" she exclaimed, touching the silky hair softly. "May I hold him for a minute?"

The maid smiled, but shook her head. "Ah, that the madame will not allow," she said.

"It cost a thousand dollars," explained Howell, eagerly, "and mamma thinks more of it than she does of us. Doesn't she, Henny?"

The small boy nodded with a finger in his mouth.

"Show her Beauty's bracelet, Fanchette," said Howell. Turning back another fold of the blanket, the maid lifted a little white paw, on which sparkled a tiny diamond bracelet. Lloyd drew a long breath of astonishment. "Some of its teeth are filled with gold," continued Howell. "We had to stay a whole week in New York while Beauty was in the dog hospital, having them filled. They could only do a little at a time. One of his tricks is to laugh so that he shows all his fillings. Laugh, Beauty!" he commanded. "Laugh, old fellow, and show your gold teeth!"

He shook a dirty finger in the poodle's face, and it obediently stretched its mouth, to show all its little gold-filled teeth.

"See!" exclaimed Howell, much pleased. "Do it again!"

But the maid interfered. "Your mother told you not to touch Beauty again. You'd have the poor little thing's mouth stretched till it had the face-ache, if you weren't watched all the time. Go away! You are a naughty boy!"

Howell's lips shot out in a sullen pout, and the maid, not knowing what he might do next, rose with the poodle in her arms and walked to the other side of the vessel.

"Wish't the little beast was dead!" he muttered. "I get scolded and punished for nothing at all whenever it is around. It and Fidelia! I haven't any use for girls and puppy-dogs!"

After this uncivil remark he waited for the angry retort which he thought would naturally follow, but to his surprise Lloyd only laughed good-naturedly. She found him amusing, even if he was rude and cross, and she could not wonder that he had such an opinion of girls, after witnessing his quarrel with

Fidelia. The boys had begun it, but she was older and could have turned it aside had she wished. And she thought it perfectly natural that he should dislike the dog if he thought his mother preferred its comfort to his.

"You'd like dogs if you could have one like my old Fritz," began Lloyd, glad of some one to talk to. Sitting down on the bench that the maid had left, she began talking of him and the pony and the other pets at Locust. At first the boys listened carelessly. Howell cracked his whip, and Henderson slapped his feet with the ends of the reins he wore. They were not used to having stories told them, except when they were being scolded, and their mother or the maid told them tales of what happens to bad little boys when they will not obey. Although Lloyd's wild ride in a hand-car with one of the two little knights began thrillingly, they listened with one foot out, ready to run at first word of the moral lecture which they thought would surely come at the end.

The poodle had a maid to make it happy and comfortable, every moment of its pampered little life. The boys had some one to see that they were properly clothed and fed, and their nursery at home looked as if a toy store had been emptied into it. But no one took any interest in their amusement. When they asked questions the answer always was, "Oh, run along and don't bother me now." There were no quiet bedtime talks for them to smooth the snarls out of the day. Their mother was always dining out or receiving company at that time, and their nurse hurried them to sleep with threats of the bugaboos under the bed that would catch them if they were not still. They suspected that the Little Colonel's stories would soon lead to a lecture on quarrelling.

Presently they forgot their fears in the interest of the tale. The youngest boy sidled a little nearer and climbed up on the end of the bench beside her. Then Howell, dragging his whip behind him, came a step closer, then another, till he too was on the bench beside her.

She had never had such a flattering audience. They never took their eyes from her face, and listened with such breathless attention that she talked on and on, wondering how long she could hold their interest.

"They listen to me just as people do to Betty," she thought, proudly. An hour went by, and half of another, and the bugle blew the first dinner-call.

"Go on," demanded Howell, edging closer. "We ain't hungry. Are we, Henny?"

"But I must go and get ready for dinner," said Lloyd, rising.

"Will you tell us some more to-morrow?" begged Howell, holding her skirts with his dirty little hand.

"Yes, yes," promised Lloyd, laughing and breaking loose from his hold. "I'll tell you as many stories as you want."

It was a rash promise, for next day, no sooner had she finished breakfast and started to take her morning walk around the deck with her father, than the boys were at her heels. They were eating bananas as they staggered along, and as fast as one disappeared another was dragged out of their blouses, which seemed pouched out all around their waists with an inexhaustible supply. Up and down they followed her, until Papa Jack began to laugh, and ask what she had done to tame the little savages.

As soon as she stopped at her chair they dropped down on the floor, tailor-fashion, waiting for her to begin. Their devotion amused her at first, and gratified her later, when the English woman who had complained of their manners stopped to speak to her.

"You are a real little 'good Samaritan,'" she said, "to keep those two nuisances quiet. The passengers owe you a vote of thanks. It is very sweet of you, my dear, to sacrifice yourself for others in that way."

Lloyd grew very red. She had not looked upon it as a sacrifice. She had been amusing herself. But after awhile story-telling did become very tiresome as a steady occupation. She groaned whenever she saw the boys coming toward her.

Fidelia joined them on several occasions, but her appearance was always the signal for a quarrel to begin. Not until one morning when the boys were locked in their stateroom for punishment, did she have a chance to speak to Lloyd by herself.

"The boys opened a port-hole this morning," explained Fidelia. "They had been forbidden to touch it. Poor Beauty was asleep on the couch just under it, and a big wave sloshed over him and nearly drowned him. He was soaked through. It gave him a chill, and mamma is in a terrible way about him. Howl and Henny told Fanchette they wanted him to drown. That's why they did it. They will be locked up all morning. I should think that you'd be glad. I don't see how you stand them tagging after you all the time. They are the meanest boys I ever knew."

"They are not mean to me," said Lloyd. "I can't help feelin' sorry for them." Then she stopped abruptly, with a blush, feeling that was not a polite thing to say to the boys' sister.

"I'm sure I don't see why you should feel sorry for them," said Fidelia, angrily. At which the Little Colonel was more embarrassed than ever. She could not tell Fidelia that it was because a little poodle received the fondling and attention that belonged to them, and that it was Fidelia's continual faultfinding and nagging that made the boys tease her. So after a pause she changed the subject by asking her what she wanted most to see in Europe.

"Nothing!" answered Fidelia. "I wouldn't give a penny to see all the old ruins and cathedrals and picture galleries in the world. The only reason that I care to go abroad is to be able to say I have been to those places when the other girls brag about what they've seen. What do you want to see?"

"Oh, thousands of things!" exclaimed Lloyd. "There are the châteaux where kings and queens have lived, and the places that are in the old songs, like Bonnie Doon, and London Bridge, and Twickenham Ferry. I want to see Denmark, because Hans Christian Andersen lived there, and wrote his fairy tales, and London, because Dickens and Little Nell lived there. But I think I shall enjoy Switzerland most. We expect to stay there a long time.

It is such a brave little country. Papa has told me
a great deal about its heroes. He is going to take
me to see the Lion of Lucerne, and to Altdorf,
under the lime-tree, where William Tell shot the
apple. I love that story."

"Well, aren't you *queer!*" exclaimed Fidelia,
opening her eyes wide and looking at Lloyd as if she
were some sort of a freak. It was her tone and
look that were offensive, more than her words.
Lloyd was furious.

"No, I am *not* queah, Miss Sattawhite!" she
exclaimed, moving away much ruffled. As she
flounced toward the cabin, her eyes very bright and
her cheeks very red, she looked back with an indignant glance. "I wish now that I'd told her why I'm
sorry for Howl and Henny. I'd be sorry for anybody
that had such a rude sistah!"

But there were other children on the vessel whose
acquaintance Lloyd made before the week was over.
She played checkers and quoits with the boys, and
paper dolls with the girls, and one sunny morning
she was invited to join the group under the stairs,
where she heard the story of the white prince from
beginning to end, and found out why he vanished.

Those were happy days on the big steamer, despite the fact that Howl and Henny haunted her

like two hungry little shadows. Sometimes the captain himself came down and walked with her. The Shermans sat at his table, and he had grown quite fond of the little Kentucky girl with her soft Southern accent. As they paced the deck hand in hand, he told her marvellous tales of the sea, till she grew to love the ship and the heaving water world around them, and wished that they might sail on and on, and never come to land until the end of the summer.

CHAPTER III.

LLOYD MEETS HERO

IT was July when they reached Switzerland. After three weeks of constant travel, it seemed good to leave boats and railroads for awhile, and stop to rest in the clean old town of Geneva. The windows of the big hotel dining-room looked out on the lake, and the Little Colonel, sitting at breakfast the morning after their arrival, could scarcely eat for watching the scene outside.

Gay little pleasure boats flashed back and forth on the sparkling water. The quay and bridge were thronged with people. From open windows down the street came the tinkle of pianos, and out on the pier, where a party of tourists were crowding on to one of the excursion steamers, a band was playing its merriest holiday music.

Far away in the distance she could see the shining snow crown of Mont Blanc, and it gave her an odd feeling, as if she were living in a geography lesson, to know that she was bounded on one side by the famous Alpine mountain, and on the other by the River Rhône, whose source she had often traced on the map. The sunshine, the music, and the gay crowds made it seem to Lloyd as if the whole world were out for a holiday, and she ate her melon and listened to the plans for the day with the sensation that something very delightful was about to happen.

"We'll go shopping this morning," said Mrs. Sherman. "I want Lloyd to see some of those wonderful music boxes they make here; the dancing bears, and the musical hand-mirrors; the chairs that play when you sit down in them, and the beer-mugs that begin a tune when you lift them up."

Lloyd's face dimpled with pleasure, and she began to ask eager questions. "Couldn't we take one to Mom Beck, mothah? A lookin'-glass that would play 'Kingdom Comin', when she picked it up? It would surprise her so she would think it was bewitched, and she'd shriek the way she does when a cattapillah gets on her."

Lloyd laughed so heartily at the recollection, that an old gentleman sitting at an opposite table smiled in sympathy. He had been watching the child ever since she came into the dining-room, interested in every look and gesture. He was a dignified old French soldier, tall and broad-shouldered, with gray

hair and a fierce-looking gray moustache drooping
heavily over his mouth. But the eyes under his
shaggy brows were so kind and gentle that the
shyest child or the sorriest waif of a stray dog would
claim him for a friend at first glance.

The Little Colonel was so busy watching the
scene from the window that she did not see him
until he had finished his breakfast and rose from
the table. As he came toward them on his way to
the door, she whispered, "Look, mothah! He has
only one arm, like grandfathah. I wondah if he
was a soldiah, too. Why is he bowing to Papa
Jack?"

"I met him last night in the office," explained her
father, when the old gentleman had passed out of
hearing. "We got into conversation over the dog
he had with him — a magnificent St. Bernard, that
had been trained as a war dog, to go out with the
ambulances to hunt for dead and wounded soldiers.
Major Pierre de Vaux is the old man's name. He
served many years in the French army, but was retired
after the siege of Strasburg. The clerk told me that it
was there that the Major lost his arm, and received his
country's medal for some act of bravery. He is well
known here in Geneva, where he comes every summer
for a few weeks."

"Oh, I hope I'll see the war dog!" cried the Little Colonel. "What do you suppose his name is?"

The waiter, who was changing their plates, could not resist this temptation to show off the little English he knew. "Hes name is *Hero*, mademoiselle," he answered. "He vair smart dog. He know *evair* sing somebody say to him, same as a person."

"You'll probably see him as we go out to the carriage," said Mr. Sherman. "He follows the Major constantly."

As soon as breakfast was over, Mrs. Sherman went up to her room for her hat. Lloyd, who had worn hers down to breakfast, wandered out into the hall to wait for her. There was a tall, carved chair standing near the elevator, and Lloyd climbed into it. To her great confusion, something inside of it gave a loud click as she seated herself, and began to play. It played so loudly that Lloyd was both startled and embarrassed. It seemed to her that every one in the hotel must hear the noise, and know that she had started it.

"Silly old thing!" she muttered, as with a very red face she slipped down and walked hurriedly away. She intended to go into the reading-room, but in her confusion turned to the left instead of the right, and

ran against some one coming out of the hotel office.
It was the Major.

"Oh, I beg your pahdon!" she cried, blushing
still more. From the twinkle in his eye she was
sure that he had witnessed her mortifying encounter
with the musical chair. But his first words made
her forget her embarrassment. He spoke in the best
of English, but with a slight accent that Lloyd
thought very odd and charming.

"Ah, it is Mr. Sherman's little daughter. He
told me last night that you had come to Switzerland
because it was a land of heroes, and he was sure that
you would be especially interested in mine. So
come, Hero, my brave fellow, and be presented to
the little American lady. Give her your paw,
sir!"

He stepped aside to let the great creature past
him, and Lloyd uttered an exclamation of delight, he
was so unusually large and beautiful. His curly coat
of tawny yellow was as soft as silk, and a great ruff
of white circled his neck like a collar. His breast
was white, too, and his paws, and his eyes had a
wistful, human look that went straight to Lloyd's
heart. She shook the offered paw, and then im-
pulsively threw her arms around his neck, exclaiming, "Oh, you deah old fellow! I can't

help lovin' you. You're the beautifulest dog I evah
saw ! "

He understood the caress, if not the words, for he
reached up to touch her cheek with his tongue, and
wagged his tail as if he were welcoming a long-lost
friend. Just then Mrs. Sherman stepped out of the
elevator. " Good-bye, Hero," said the Little Colonel.
"I must go now, but I hope I'll see you when I come
back." Nodding good-bye to the Major, she followed
her mother out to the street, where her father stood
waiting beside an open carriage.

Lloyd enjoyed the drive that morning as they spun
along beside the river, up and down the strange
streets with the queer foreign signs over the shop
doors. Once, as they drove along the quay, they
met the Major and the dog, and in response to a
courtly bow, the Little Colonel waved her hand and
smiled. The empty sleeve recalled her grandfather,
and gave her a friendly feeling for the old soldier.
She looked back at Hero as long as she could see a
gilmpse of his white and yellow curls.

It was nearly noon when they stopped at a place
where Mrs. Sherman wanted to leave an enamelled
belt-buckle to be repaired. Lloyd was not interested
in the show-cases, and could not understand the conversation her father and mother were having with

the shopkeeper about enamelling. So, saying that she would go out and sit in the carriage until they were ready to come, she slipped away.

She liked to watch the stir of the streets. It was interesting to guess what the foreign signs meant, and to listen to the strange speech around her. Besides, there was a band playing somewhere down the street, and children were tugging at their nurses' hands to hurry them along. Some carried dolls dressed in the quaint costumes of Swiss peasants, and some had balloons. A man with a bunch of them like a cluster of great red bubbles, had just sold out on the corner.

So she sat in the sunshine, looking around her with eager, interested eyes. The coachman, high up on his box, seemed as interested as herself; at least, he sat up very straight and stiff. But it was only his back that Lloyd saw. He had been at a fête the night before. There seems to be always a holiday in Geneva. He had stayed long at the merry-making and had taken many mugs of beer. They made him drowsy and stupid. The American gentleman and his wife stayed long in the enameller's shop. He could scarcely keep his eyes open. Presently, although he never moved a muscle of his back and sat up stiff and straight as a poker, he was sound asleep, and the reins in his grasp slipped lower and lower and lower.

The horse was an old one, stiffened and jaded by much hard travel, but it had been a mettlesome one in its younger days, with the recollection of many exciting adventures. Now, although it seemed half asleep, dreaming, maybe, of the many jaunts it had taken with other American tourists, or wondering if it were not time for it to have its noonday nose-bag, it was really keeping one eye open, nervously watching some painters on the sidewalk. They were putting up a scaffold against a building, in order that they might paint the cornice.

Presently the very thing happened that the old horse had been expecting. A heavy board fell from the scaffold with a crash, knocking over a ladder, which fell into the street in front of the frightened animal. Now the old horse had been in several runaways. Once it had been hurt by a falling ladder, and it had never recovered from its fear of one. As this one fell just under it's nose, all the old fright and pain that caused its first runaway seemed to come back to its memory. In a frenzy of terror it reared, plunged forward, then suddenly turned and dashed down the street.

The plunge and sudden turn threw the sleeping

coachman from the box to the street. With the lines dragging at its heels, the frightened horse sped on. The Little Colonel, clutching frantically at the seat in front of her, screamed at the horse to stop. She had been used to driving ever since she was big enough to grasp the reins, and she felt that if she could only reach the dragging lines, she could control the horse. But that was impossible. All she could do was to cling to the seat as the carriage whirled dizzily around corners, and wonder how many more frightful turns it would make before she should be thrown out.

The white houses on either side seemed racing past them. Nurses ran, screaming, to the pavements, dragging the baby-carriages out of the way. Dogs barked and teams were jerked hastily aside. Some one dashed out of a shop and threw his arms up in front of the horse to stop it, but, veering to one side, it only plunged on the faster.

Lloyd's hat blew off. Her face turned white with a sickening dread, and her breath began to come in frightened sobs. On and on they went, and, as the scenes of a lifetime will be crowded into a moment in the memory of a drowning man, so a thousand things came flashing into Lloyd's mind. She saw the locust avenue all white and sweet in blossom time, and thought, with a strange thrill of self-pity, that she would never ride under its white arch again. Then she saw Betty's face on the pillow, as she had lain with bandaged eyes, telling in her tremulous little voice the story of the Road of the Loving Heart. Queerly enough, with that came the thought of Howl and Henny, and she had time to be glad that she had amused them on the voyage, and made them happy. Then came her mother's face, and Papa Jack's. In a few moments, she told herself, they would be picking up her poor, broken, lifeless little body from the street. How horribly they would feel. And then — she screamed and shut her eyes. The carriage had dashed into something that tore off a wheel. There was a crash — a sound as of splintering wood. But it did not stop their mad flight. With a horrible bumping motion that nearly threw her from the carriage at every jolt, they still kept on.

They were on the quay now. The noon sun on the water flashed into her eyes like the blinding light thrown back from a looking-glass. Then something white and yellow darted from the crowd on the pavement, and catching the horse by the bit, swung on heavily. The horse dragged along for a few paces, and came to a halt, trembling like a leaf.

A wild hurrah went up from both sides of the street, and the Little Colonel, as she was lifted out white and trembling, saw that it was a huge St. Bernard that the crowd was cheering.

"Oh, it's H-Hero!" she cried, with chattering teeth. "How did he get here?" But no one understood her question. The faces she looked into, while beaming with friendly interest, were all foreign. The eager exclamations on all sides were uttered in a foreign tongue. There was no one to take her home, and in her fright she could not remember the name of their hotel. But in the midst of her confusion a hearty sentence in English sounded in her ear, and a strong arm caught her up in a fatherly embrace. It was the Major who came pushing through the crowd to reach her. Her grandfather himself could not have been more welcome just at that time, and her tears came fast when she found herself in his friendly shelter. The shock had been a terrible one.

"Come, dear child!" he exclaimed, gently, patting her shoulder. "Courage! We are almost at the hotel. See, it is on the corner, there. The father and mother will soon be here."

Wiping her eyes, he led her across the street, explaining as he went how it happened that he and the dog were on the street when she passed. They had been in the gardens all morning and were going home to lunch, when they heard the clatter of the runaway far down the street. The Major could not see who was in the carriage, only that it appeared to be a child. He was too old a man, and with his one arm too helpless to attempt to stop it, but he remembered that Hero had once shared the training of some collies for police service, before it had been decided to use him as an ambulance dog. They were taught to spring at the bridles of escaping horses.

"I was doubtful if Hero remembered those early lessons," said the Major, "but I called out to him sharply, for the love of heaven to stop it if he could, and that instant he was at the horse's head, hanging on with all his might. Bravo, old fellow!" he continued, turning to the dog as he spoke. "We are proud of you this day!"

They were in the corridor of the hotel now, and the Little Colonel, kneeling beside Hero and putting her arms around his neck, finished her sobbing with her fair little face laid fondly against his silky coat.

"Oh, you deah, deah old Hero," she said. "You saved me, and I'll love you fo' evah and evah!"

The crowd was still in front of the hotel, and the corridor full of excited servants and guests, when Mr.

and Mrs. Sherman hurried in. They had taken the first carriage they could hail and driven as fast as possible in the wake of the runaway. Mrs. Sherman was trembling so violently that she could scarcely stand, when they reached the hotel. The clerk who ran out to assure them of the Little Colonel's safety was loud in his praises of the faithful St. Bernard.

Hero had known many masters. Any one in the uniform of the army had once had authority over him. He had been taught to obey many voices. Many hands had fed and fondled him, but no hand had ever lain quite so tenderly on his head, as the Little Colonel's. No one had ever looked into his eyes so gratefully as she, and no voice had ever thrilled him with as loving tones as hers, as she knelt there beside him, calling him all the fond endearing names she knew. He understood far better than if he had been human, that she loved him. Eagerly licking her hands and wagging his tail, he told her as plainly as a dog can talk that henceforth he would be one of her best and most faithful of friends.

If petting and praise and devoted attention could spoil a dog, Hero's head would certainly have been turned that day, for friends and strangers alike made much of him. A photographer came to take his picture for the leading daily paper. Before nightfall his story was repeated in every home in Geneva. No servant in the hotel but took a personal pride in him or watched his chance to give him a sly sweetmeat or a caress. But being a dog instead of a human, the attention only made him the more lovable, for it made him feel that it was a kind world he lived in and everybody was his friend.

It was after lunch that the Little Colonel came upstairs carrying the diary, now half-filled with the record of their journeying.

"Put it all down in the book, Papa Jack," she demanded. "I'll nevah forget to my dyin' day, but I want it written down heah in black and white that Hero saved me!"

CHAPTER IV.

HERO'S STORY

LATE that afternoon the Major sat out in the shady courtyard of the hotel, where vines, potted plants, and a fountain made a cool green garden spot. He was thinking of his little daughter, who had been dead many long years. The American child, whom his dog had rescued from the runaway in the morning, was wonderfully like her. She had the same fair hair, he thought, that had been his little Christine's great beauty; the same delicate, wild-rose pink in her cheeks, the same mischievous smile dimpling her laughing face. But Christine's eyes had not been a starry hazel like the Little Colonel's. They were blue as the flax-flowers she used to gather — thirty, was it? No, forty years ago.

As he counted the years, the thought came to him like a pain that he was an old, old man now, all alone in the world, save for a dog, and a niece whom he scarcely knew and seldom saw.

As he sat there with his head bowed down, dreaming over his past, the Little Colonel came out into the courtyard. She had dressed early and gone down to the reading-room to wait until her mother was ready for dinner, but catching sight of the Major through the long glass doors, she laid down her book. The lonely expression of his furrowed face, the bowed head, and the empty sleeve appealed to her strongly.

"I believe I'll go out and talk to him," she thought. "If grandfathah were away off in a strange land by himself like that, I'd want somebody to cheer him up."

It is always good to feel that one is welcome, and Lloyd was glad that she had ventured into the courtyard, when she saw the smile that lighted the Major's face at sight of her, and when the dog, rising at her approach, came forward joyfully wagging his tail.

The conversation was easy to begin, with Hero for a subject. There were many things she wanted to know about him : how he happened to belong to the Major ; what country he came from ; why he was called a St. Bernard, and if the Major had ever owned any other dogs.

After a few questions it all came about as she had hoped it would. The old man settled himself back in his chair, thought a moment, and then began at the first of his acquaintance with St. Bernard dogs, as if he were reading a story from a book.

"Away up in the Alpine Mountains, too high for trees to grow, where there is only bare rock and snow and cutting winds, climbs the road that is known as the Great St. Bernard Pass. It is an old, old road. The Celts crossed it when they invaded Italy. The Roman legions crossed it when they marched out to subdue Gaul and Germany. Ten hundred years ago the Saracen robbers hid among its rocks to waylay unfortunate travellers. You will read about all that in your history sometime, and about the famous march Napoleon made across it on his way to Marengo. But the most interesting fact about the road to me, is that for over seven hundred years there has been a monastery high up on the bleak mountain-top, called the monastery of St. Bernard.

"Once, when I was travelling through the Alps, I stopped there one cold night, almost frozen. The good monks welcomed me to their hospice, as they do all strangers who stop for food and shelter, and treated me as kindly as if I had been a brother. In the morning one of them took me out to the kennels, and showed me the dogs that are trained to look for travellers in the snow. You may imagine with what pleasure I followed him, and listened to the tales he told me.

"He said there is not as much work for the dogs now as there used to be years ago. Since the hospice has been connected with the valley towns by telephone, travellers can inquire about the state of the weather and the paths, before venturing up the dangerous mountain passes. Still, the storms begin with little warning sometimes, and wayfarers are overtaken by them and lost in the blinding snowfall. The paths fill suddenly, and but for the dogs many would perish."

"Oh, I know," interrupted Lloyd, eagerly. "There is a story about them in my old third readah, and a pictuah of a big St. Bernard dog with a flask tied around his neck, and a child on his back."

"Yes," answered the Major, "it is quite probable that that was a picture of the dog they called Barry. He was with the good monks for twelve years, and in that time saved the lives of forty travellers. There is a monument erected to him in Paris in the cemetery for dogs. The sculptor carved that picture into the stone, the noble animal with a child on his back, as if he were in the act of carrying it to the hospice. Twelve years is a long time for a dog to suffer such hardship and exposure. Night after night he plunged out alone into the deep snow and the darkness, barking at the top of his voice to attract the attention of lost travellers. Many a time he dropped into the drifts exhausted, with scarcely enough strength left to drag himself back to the hospice.

"Forty lives saved is a good record. You may be sure that in his old age Barry was tenderly cared for. The monks gave him a pension and sent him to Berne, where the climate is much warmer. When he died, a taxidermist preserved his skin, and he was placed in the museum at Berne, where he stands to this day, I am told, with the little flask around his neck. I saw him there one time, and although Barry was only a dog, and I an officer in my country's service, I stood with uncovered head before him. For he was as truly a hero and served human kind as nobly as if he had fallen on the field of battle.

"He had been trained like a soldier to his duty, and no matter how the storms raged on the mountains, how dark the night, or how dangerous the paths that led along the slippery precipices, at the word of command he sprang to obey. Only a dumb beast, some people would call him, guided only by brute instinct, but in his shaggy old body beat a loving heart, loyal to his master's command, and faithful to his duty.

"As I stood there gazing into the kind old face, I thought of the time when I lay wounded on the field of Strasburg. How glad I would have been to have seen some dog like Barry come bounding to my aid! I had fallen in a thicket, where the ambulance corps did not discover me until next day. I lay there all that black night, wild with pain, groaning for water. I could see the lanterns of the ambulances as they moved about searching for the wounded among the many dead, but was too faint from loss of blood to raise my head and shout for help. They told me afterward that, if my wound could have received immediate attention, perhaps my arm might have been saved.

"But only a keen sense of smell could have traced me in the dense thicket where I lay. No one had thought of training dogs for ambulance service then. The men did their best, but they were only men, and I was overlooked until it was too late to save my arm.

"Well, as I said, I stood and looked at Barry, wondering if it were not possible to train dogs for rescue work on battle-fields as well as in mountain passes. The more I thought of it, the more my longing grew to make such an attempt. I read everything I could find about trained dogs, visited

kennels where collies and other intelligent sheep-
dogs were kept, and corresponded with many people
about it. Finally I found a man who was as much
interested in the subject as I. Herr Bungartz is
his name. To him chiefly belongs the credit for
the development of the use of ambulance dogs, to aid
the wounded on the field of battle. He is now at the
head of a society to which I belong. It has over
a thousand members, including many princes and
generals.

" We furnish the money that supports the kennels,
and the dogs are bred and trained free for the army.
Now for the last eight years it has been my greatest
pleasure to visit the kennels, where as many as fifty
dogs are kept constantly in training. It was on my
last visit that I got Hero. His leg had been hurt
in some accident on the training field. It was
thought that he was too much disabled to ever do
good service again, so they allowed me to take him.
Two old cripples, I suppose they thought we were,
comrades in misfortune.

" That was nearly a year ago. I took him to an
eminent surgeon, told him his history, and interested
him in his case. He treated him so successfully,
that now, as you see, the leg is entirely well. Sometimes I feel that it is my duty to give him back to

the service, although I paid for the rearing of a fine Scotch collie in his stead. He is so unusually intelligent and well trained. But it would be hard to part with such a good friend. Although I have had him less than a year, he seems very much attached to me, and I have grown more fond of him than I would have believed possible. I am an old man now, and I think he understands that he is all I have. Good Hero! He knows he is a comfort to his old master!"

At the sound of his name, uttered in a sad voice, the great dog got up and laid his head on the Major's knee, looking wistfully into his face.

"Of co'se you oughtn't to give him back!" cried the Little Colonel. "If he were mine, I wouldn't give him up for the president, or the emperor, or the czar, or *anybody!*"

"But for the soldiers, the poor wounded soldiers!" suggested the Major.

Lloyd hesitated, looking from the dog to the empty sleeve above it. "Well," she declared, at last, "I wouldn't give him up while the country is at peace. I'd wait till the last minute, until there was goin' to be an awful battle, and then I'd make them promise to let me have him again when the wah was ovah. Just the minute it was ovah. It would be like givin' away part of your family to give away Hero."

Suddenly the Major spoke to the dog in French, a quick, sharp sentence that Lloyd could not understand. But Hero, without an instant's hesitation, bounded from the courtyard, where they sat, into the hall of the hotel. Through the glass doors she could see him leaping up the stairs, and, almost before the Major could explain that he had sent him for the shoulder-bags he wore in service, the dog was back with them grasped firmly in his mouth.

"Now the flask," said the Major. While the dog obeyed the second order, he opened the bags for Lloyd to examine them. They were marked with a red cross in a square of white, and contained rolls of bandages, from which any man, able to use his arms, could help himself until his rescuer brought further aid.

The flask which Hero brought was marked in the same way, and the Major buckled it to his collar, saying, as he fastened first that and then the shoulder-bags in place, "When a dog is in training, soldiers, pretending to be dead or wounded, are hidden in the woods or ravines and he is taught to find a fallen body, and to bark loudly. If the soldier is in some place too remote for his voice to bring aid, the dog seizes a cap, a handkerchief, or a belt, — any article of the man's clothing which he can pick up, — and dashes back to the nearest ambulance."

"What a lovely game that would make!" exclaimed Lloyd. "Do you suppose that I could train the two Bobs to do that? We often play soldiah at Locust. Now, what is it you say to Hero when you want him to hunt the men? Let me see if he'll mind me."

The Major repeated the command.

"But I can't speak French," she said in dismay. "What is it in English?"

"Hero can't understand anything in English," said the Major, laughing at the perplexed expression that crept into the Little Colonel's face.

"How funny!" she exclaimed. "I nevah thought of that befo'. I supposed of co'se that all animals were English. Anyway, Hero comes when I call him, and wags his tail when I speak, just as if he undahstands every word."

"It is the kindness in your voice he understands, and the smile in your eyes, the affection in your caress. That language is the same the world over, to men and animals alike. But he never would start out to hunt the wounded soldiers unless you gave this command. Let me hear if you can say it after me."

Lloyd tripped over some of the rough sounds as she repeated the sentence, but tried it again and again until the Major cried "Bravo! You shall have more lessons in French, dear child, until you can give the command so well that Hero shall obey you as he does me."

Then he began talking of Christine, her fair hair, her blue eyes, her playful ways; and Lloyd, listening, drew him on with many questions, till the little French maiden seemed to stand pictured before her, her hands filled with the lovely spring flowers of the motherland.

Suddenly the Major arose, bowing courteously, for Mrs. Sherman, seeing them from the doorway, had smiled and started toward them. Springing up, Lloyd ran to meet her.

"Mothah," she whispered, "please ask the Majah to sit at ou' table to-night at dinnah. He's such a deah old man, and tells such interestin' things, and he's lonesome. The tears came into his eyes when he talked about his little daughtah. She was just my age when she died, mothah, and he thinks she looked like me."

The Major's courtly manner and kind face had already aroused Mrs. Sherman's interest. His empty sleeve reminded her of her father. His loneliness appealed to her sympathy, and his kindness to her little daughter had won her deepest appreciation. She turned with a cordial smile to repeat Lloyd's invitation, which was gladly accepted.

That was the beginning of a warm friendship. From that time he was included in their plans. Now, in nearly all their excursions and drives, there were four in the party instead of three, and five, very often. Whenever it was possible, Hero was with them. He and the Little Colonel often went out together alone. It grew to be a familiar sight in the town, the graceful fair-haired child and the big tawny St. Bernard, walking side by side along the quay. She was not afraid to venture anywhere with such a guard. As for Hero, he followed her as gladly as he did his master.

CHAPTER V.

THE RED CROSS OF GENEVA

A WEEK after the runaway the handsomest collar that could be bought in town was fastened around Hero's neck. It had taken a long time to get it, for Mr. Sherman went to many shops before he found material that he considered good enough for the rescuer of his little daughter. Then the jeweller had to keep it several days while he engraved an inscription on the gold name-plate — an inscription that all who read might know what happened on a certain July day in the old Swiss town of Geneva. On the under side of the collar was a stout link like the one on his old one, to which the flask could be fastened when he was harnessed for service, and on the upper side, finely wrought in enamel, was a red cross on a white square.

"Papa Jack!" exclaimed Lloyd, examining it with interest, "that is the same design that is on his blanket and shouldah-bags. Why, it's just like the Swiss flag!" she cried, looking out at the banner floating from the pier. "Only the colours are turned around. The flag has a white cross on a red ground, and this is a red cross on a white ground. Why did you have it put on the collah, Papa Jack?"

"Because he is a Red Cross dog," answered her father.

"No, Papa Jack. Excuse me for contradictin', but the Majah said he was a St. Bernard dog."

Mr. Sherman laughed, but before he could explain he was called to the office to answer a telegram. When he returned Lloyd had disappeared to find the Major, and ask about the symbol on the collar. She found him in his favourite seat near the fountain, in the shady courtyard. Perching on a bench near by with Hero for a foot-stool, she asked, "Majah, is Hero a St. Bernard or a Red Cross dog?"

"He is both," answered the Major, smiling at her puzzled expression. "He is the first because he belongs to that family of dogs, and he is the second because he was adopted by the Red Cross Association, and trained for its service. You know what that is, of course."

Still Lloyd looked puzzled. She shook her head. "No, I nevah heard of it. Is it something Swiss or French?"

"Never heard of it!" repeated the Major. He

spoke in such a surprised tone that his voice sounded gruff and loud, and Lloyd almost jumped. The harshness was so unexpected.

"Think again, child," he said, sternly. "Surely you have been told, at least, of your brave country-woman who is at the head of the organisation in America, who nursed not only the wounded of your own land, but followed the Red Cross of mercy on many foreign battle-fields!"

"Oh, a hospital nurse!" said Lloyd, wrinkling her forehead and trying to think. "Miss Alcott was one. Everybody knows about her, and her 'Hospital Sketches' are lovely."

"No! no!" exclaimed the Major, impatiently. Lloyd, feeling from his tone that ignorance on this subject was something he could not excuse, tried again.

"I've heard of Florence Nightingale. In one of my books at home, a *Chatterbox*, I think, there is a picture of her going through a hospital ward. Mothah told me how good she was to the soldiahs, and how they loved her. They even kissed her shadow on the wall as she passed. They were so grateful."

"Ah, yes," murmured the old man. "Florence Nightingale will live long in song and story. An angel of mercy she was, through all the horrors of the Crimean War; but she was an English woman, my dear. The one I mean is an American, and her name ought to go down in history with the bravest of its patriots and the most honoured of its benefactors. I learned to know her first in that long siege at Strasburg. She nursed me there, and I have followed her career with grateful interest ever since, noting with admiration all that she has done for her country and humanity the world over.

"If America ever writes a woman's name in her temple of fame, dear child (I say it with uncovered head), that one should be the name of *Clara Barton*."

The old soldier lifted his hat as he spoke, and replaced it so solemnly that Lloyd felt very uncomfortable, as if she were in some way to blame for not knowing and admiring this Red Cross nurse of whom she had never heard. Her face flushed, and much embarrassed, she drew the toe of her slipper along Hero's back, answering, in an abused tone:

"But, Majah, how could I be expected to know anything about her? There is nothing in ou' schoolbooks, and nobody told me, and Papa Jack won't let me read the newspapahs, they're so full of horrible murdahs and things. So how could I evah find out?

I couldn't learn *everything* in twelve yeahs, and
that's all the longah I've lived."

The Major laughed. "Forgive me, little one!"
he cried, seeing the distress and embarrassment in
her face. "A thousand pardons! The fault is not
yours, but your country's, that it has not taught its
children to honour its benefactor as she deserves. I
am glad that it has been given to me to tell you the
story of one of the most beautiful things that ever
happened in Switzerland — the founding of the Red
Cross. You will remember it with greater interest,
I am sure, because, while I talk, the cross of the
Swiss flag floats over us, and it was here in this old
town of Geneva the merciful work had its beginning."

Lloyd settled herself to listen, still stroking
Hero's back with her slipper toe.

"He was my friend, Henri Durant, and in the old
days of chivalry they would have made him knight
for the noble thought that sprang to flower in his
heart and to fruitage in so worthy a deed. He was
travelling in Italy years ago, and happening to be
near the place where the battle of Solferino was
fought, he was so touched by the sufferings of the
wounded that he stopped to help care for them in
the hospitals. The sights he saw there were hor-

rible.   The wounded men could not be cared for properly.   They died by the hundreds, because there were not enough nurses and surgeons and food.

"It moved him to write a book which was translated into several languages.   People of many countries became interested and were aroused to a desire to do something to relieve the deadly consequences of war.   Then he called a meeting of all the nations of Europe.   That was over thirty years ago.   Sixteen of the great powers sent men to represent them.   They met here in Geneva and signed a treaty.   One by one other countries followed their example, until now forty governments are pledged to keep the promises of the Red Cross.

"They chose that as their flag in compliment to Switzerland, where the movement was started.   You see they are the same except that the colours are reversed.

"Now, according to that treaty, wherever the Red Cross goes, on sea or on land, it means peace and safety for the wounded soldiers.   In the midst of the bloodiest battle, no matter who is hurt, Turk or Russian, Japanese or Spaniard, Armenian or Arab, he is bound to be protected and cared for. No nurse, surgeon, or ambulance bearing that Red

Cross can be fired upon. They are allowed to pass wherever they are needed.

"Before the nations joined in that treaty, the worst horror of war was the fate of a wounded soldier, falling into the hands of the enemy. Better a thousand times to be killed in battle, than to be taken prisoner. Think of being left, bleeding and faint, on an enemy's field till your clothes *froze to the ground,* and no one merciful enough to give you a crust of bread or a drop of water. Think of the dying piled with the dead and left to the pitiless rays of a scorching, tropic sun. That can never happen again, thank Heaven!

"In time of peace, money and supplies are gathered and stored by each country, ready for use at the first signal of war. To show her approval, the empress became the head of the branch in Germany. Soon after the Franco-Prussian war began, and then her only daughter, the Grand Duchess Louise of Baden, turned all her beautiful castles into military hospitals, and went herself to superintend the work of relief.

"Your country did not join with us at first. You were having a terrible war at home; the one in which your grandfather fought. All this time Clara Barton was with the soldiers on their bloodiest bat-

tle-fields. When you go home, ask your grandfather
about the battles of Bull Run and Antietam, Fred-
ericksburg and the Wilderness. She was there.
She stood the strain of nursing in sixteen such awful
places, going from cot to cot among the thousands of
wounded, comforting the dying, and dragging many
a man back from the very grave by her untiring,
unselfish devotion.

"When the war was over, she spent four years
searching for the soldiers reported missing. Hundreds and hundreds of pitiful letters came to her,
giving name, regiment, and company of some son or
husband or brother, who had marched away to the
wars and never returned. These names could not
be found among the lists of the killed. They were
simply reported as 'missing'; whether dead or a
deserter, no one could tell. She had spent weeks
at Andersonville the summer after the war, identify-
ing and marking the graves there. She marked
over twelve thousand. So when these letters came
imploring her aid, she began the search, visiting the
old prisons, and trenches and hospitals, until she re-
moved from twenty thousand names the possible
suspicion that the men who bore them had been
deserters.

"No wonder that she came to Europe completely

broken down in health, so exhausted by her long, severe labours that her physicians told her she must rest several years. But hardly was she settled here in Switzerland when the Franco-Prussian war broke out, and the Red Cross sought her aid, knowing how valuable her long experience in nursing would be to them. She could not refuse their appeals, and once more started in the wake of powder smoke, and cannon's roar.

"But I'll not start on that chapter of her life, for, if I did, I would not know where to stop. It was there I met her, there she nursed me back to life; then I learned to appreciate her devotion to the cause of humankind. This second long siege against suffering made her an invalid for many years.

"The other nations wondered why America refused to join them in their humane work. All other civilised countries were willing to lend a hand. But Clara Barton knew that it was because the people were ignorant of its real purpose that they did not join the alliance, and she promised that she would devote the remainder of her life, if need be, to showing America that as long as she refused to sign that treaty, she was standing on a level with barbarous and heathen countries.

"For years she was too ill to push the work she

had set for herself. When her strength at last returned, she had to learn to walk. At last, however, she succeeded. America signed the treaty. Then, through her efforts, the American National Red Cross was organised. She was made president of it. While no war, until lately, has called for its services, the Red Cross has found plenty to do in times of great national calamities. You have had terrible fires and floods, cyclones, and scourges of yellow fever. Then too, it has taken relief to Turkey and lately has found work in Cuba.

"I know that you would like to look into Miss Barton's jewel-box. Old Emperor William himself gave her the Iron Cross of Prussia. The Grand Duke and Duchess of Baden sent her the Gold Cross of Remembrance. Medals and decorations from many sovereigns are there — the Queen of Servia, the Sultan of Turkey, the Prince of Armenia. Never has any American woman been so loved and honoured abroad, and never has an American woman been more worthy of respect at home. It must be a great joy to her now, as she sits in the evening of life, to count her jewels of remembrance, and feel that she has done so much to win the gratitude of her fellow creatures.

"You came to visit Switzerland because it is the

home of many heroes; but let me tell you, my child,
this little republic has more to show the world than
its William Tell chapels and its Lion of Lucerne. As
long as the old town of Geneva stands, the world will
not forget that here was given a universal banner of
peace, and here was signed its greatest treaty — the
treaty of the Red Cross."

As the Major stopped, the Little Colonel looked up
at the white cross floating above the pier, and then
down at the red one on Hero's collar, and drew a long
breath.

"I wish I could do something like that!" she exclaimed, earnestly. "I used to wish that I could go
out like Joan of Arc to do some great thing that
would make people write books about me, and carve
me on statues, and paint pictures and sing songs in
my honah, but I believe that now I'd rathah do something bettah than ride off to battle on a prancin'
white chargah. Thank you, Majah, for tellin' me
the story. I'm goin' for a walk now. May I take
Hero?"

A few minutes later the two were wandering along
beside the water together, the Little Colonel dreaming day-dreams of valiant deeds that she might do
some day, so that kings would send *her* a Gold Cross
of Remembrance, and men would say with uncovered

heads, as the old Major had done, " If America ever writes a woman's name in her temple of fame, that one should be the name of Lloyd Sherman — *The Little Colonel !* "

CHAPTER VI.

THE WONDER - BALL'S BEST GIFT

As the time drew near for them to move north-ward, Lloyd began counting the hours still left to her to spend with her new-found friends.

"Only two moah days, mothah," she sighed. "Only two moah times to go walking with Hero. It seems to me that I *can't* say good-bye and go away, and nevah see him again as long as I live!"

"He is going with us part of the way," answered Mrs. Sherman. "The Major told us last night that he had decided to visit his niece who lives at Zürich. We will stop first for a few days at a little town called Zug, beside a lake of the same name. There is a William Tell chapel near there that the Major wants to show us, and he will go up the Rigi with us. I think he dreads parting with you fully as much as you do from Hero. His eyes follow every movement you make. So many times in speaking of you he has called you Christine."

"I know," answered Lloyd, thoughtfully. "He

seems to mix me up with her in his thoughts, all the time. He is so old I suppose he is absent-minded. When I'm as old as he is, I won't want to travel around as he does. I'll want to settle down in some comfortable place and stay there."

" From what he said last night, I judge that this is the last time he expects to visit that part of Switzerland. When he was a little boy he used to visit his grandmother, who lived near Zug. The chalet where she lived is still standing, and he wants to see it once more, he said, before he dies."

" He must know lots of stories about the place," said Lloyd.

" He does. He has tramped all over the mountain back of the town after wild strawberries, followed the peasants to the mowing, and gone to many a fête in the village. We are fortunate to have such an interesting guide."

" I wish that Betty could be with us to hear all the stories he tells us," said Lloyd, beginning to look forward to the journey with more pleasure, now that she knew there was a prospect of being entertained by the Major. Usually she grew tired of the confinement in the little railway carriages where there were no aisles to walk up and down in, and fidgeted and yawned and asked the time of day at every station.

During the first part of the journey toward Zug, the Major had little to say. He leaned wearily back in his seat with his eyes closed much of the time. But as they began passing places that were connected with interesting scenes of his childhood, he roused himself, and pointed them out with as much enjoyment as if he were a schoolboy, coming home on his first vacation.

" See those queer little towers still left standing on the remnants of the old town wall," he said as they approached Zug. " The lake front rests on a soft, shifting substratum of sand, and there is danger, when the water is unusually low, that it may not be able to support the weight of the houses built upon it. One day, over four hundred years ago, part of the wall and some of the towers sank down into the lake with twenty-six houses.

" I have heard my grandmother tell of it, many a time, as she heard the tale from her grandmother. Many lives were lost that day, and there was a great panic. Later in the day, some one saw a cradle floating out in the lake, and when it was drawn in, there lay a baby, cooing and kicking up his heels as happily as if cradle-rides on the water were common occurrences. He was the little son of the town clerk, and grew up to be one of my ancestors. Grandmother was very fond of telling that tale, how the baby smiled on his rescuers, and what a fine, pleasant man he grew up to be, beloved by the whole village.

"It has not been much over a dozen years since another piece of the town sank down into the water. A long stretch of lake front with houses and gardens and barns was sucked under."

"How dreadful!" exclaimed Lloyd, with a shiver. "Let us go somewhere else, Papa Jack," she begged. "I don't want to sleep in a place where the bottom may drop out any minute."

Her father laughed at her fears, and the Major assured her that they would not take her to a hotel near the water's edge.

"We are going to the other side of the town, to an inn that stands close against the mountainside. The inn-keeper is an old friend of mine, who has lived here all his life."

In spite of all they said to quiet her fears, the Little Colonel was far from feeling comfortable, and took small pleasure at first in going to see the sights of the quaint little town. She was glad when they pushed away from the pier next morning, in the steamboat that was to take them across the lake to the William Tell chapel. She dreaded to return, but a handful of letters from Lloydsboro Valley, and one

apiece from Betty and Eugenia that she found awaiting her at the inn, made her forget the shifting sands
below her.   She read and re-read some of them, answered several, and then began to look for the Major
and Hero.   They were nowhere to be found.

They went away directly after lunch, her father
told her, to the chalet on the mountain back of the
town.   "You will have to be content with my
humble society," he added.   "You can't expect to
be always escorted by titled soldiers and heroes."

"Now you're teasin'," said Lloyd, with a playful
pout.   "But I do wish that the Majah had left Hero.
There are so few times left for us to go walkin'
togethah."

"I'm afraid that you look oftener at that dog than
you do at the scenery and the foreign sights that
you came over here to see," said her father, with a
smile.   "You can see dogs in Lloydsboro Valley any
day."

"But none like Hero," cried the Little Colonel,
loyally.   "And I *am* noticin' the sights, Papa Jack.   I
think there was nevah anything moah beautiful than
these mountains, and I just love it heah when it is so
sunny and still.   Listen to the goat-bells tinklin'
away up yondah where that haymakah is climbing
with a pack of hay tied on his shouldahs!   And how

deep and sweet the church-bell sounds down heah in the valley as it tolls across the watah! The lake looks as blue as the sapphires in mothah's necklace. The pictuah it makes for me is one of the loveliest things that my wondah-ball has unrolled. Nobody could have a bettah birthday present than this trip has been. The only thing about it that has made me unhappy for a minute is that I must leave Hero and nevah see him again. He follows me just as well now as he does his mastah."

The Major came back from his long climb up the mountain, very tired. "It is more than I should have undertaken the first day," he said, "but back here in the scenes of my boyhood I find it hard to realise that I am an old, old man. I'll be rested in the morning, however, ready for whatever comes."

But in the morning he was still much exhausted, and came down-stairs leaning heavily on his cane. He asked to be excused from going up on the Rigi with them. He said that he would stay at home and sit in the sun and rest. They offered to postpone the trip, but he insisted on their going without him. They must be moving on to Zürich, soon, he reminded them, and they might not have another day of such perfect weather, for the excursion.

Hero stood looking from the Major in his chair, to

the Little Colonel, standing with her hat and jacket on, ready to start. He could not understand why he and his master should be left behind, and walked from one to the other, wagging his tail and looking up questioningly into their faces.

"Go, if you wish," said the Major, kindly patting his head. "Go and take good care of thy little Christine. Let no harm befall her this day!" The dog bounded away as if glad of the permission, but at the door turned back, and seeing that the Major was not following, picked up his hat in his mouth. Then, carrying it back to the Major, stood looking up into his master's face, wagging his tail.

The Major took the hat and laid it on the table beside him. "No, not to-day, good friend," he said, smiling at the dog's evident wish to have him go also. "You may go without me, this time. Call him, Christine, if you wish his company."

"Come Hero, come on," called Lloyd. "It's all right."

The Major waved his hand toward her, saying, "Go, Hero. Guard her well and bring her back safely. The dear little Christine!" The name was uttered almost in a whisper.

With a quick, short bark, Hero started after the Little Colonel, staying so closely by her side that they entered the train together before the guard could protest.   If he could have resisted the appealing look in the Little Colonel's eyes as she threw an arm protectingly around Hero's neck, he could not find it in his heart to refuse the silver that Papa Jack slipped into his hand ; so for once the two comrades travelled side by side.   Hero sat next the window, and looked out anxiously, as the little mountain engine toiled up the steep ascent, nearer and nearer to the top.

It was noon when they reached the hotel on the summit where they stopped for lunch.

" How solemn it makes you feel to be up so high above all the world ! " said Lloyd, in an awed tone, as they walked around that afternoon, and took turns looking through the great telescope, at the valley spread out like a map below them.

" How tiny the lake looks, and the town is like a toy village !   I thought that the top of a mountain went up to a fine point like a church steeple, and that there wouldn't be a place to stand on when you got there.   Seems that way when you look up at it from the valley.   It doesn't seem possible that it is big enough to have hotels built on it and lots and lots of room left ovah.   When the Majah said to Hero, in such a solemn way, ' Take good care of thy little Christine, let no harm befall her this day,' I thought maybe he wanted Hero to hold my dress in his teeth, so that I couldn't fall off."

Mrs. Sherman laughed and Mr. Sherman said, "Do you know that you are actually up above the clouds? What seems to be mist, rolling over the valley down there like a dense fog, is really cloud. In a short time we shall not be able to see through it."

"Oh, oh!" cried the Little Colonel, in astonishment. "Really, Papa Jack? I always thought that if I could get up into the clouds I could reach out and touch the moon and the stars. Of co'se I know bettah now, but I should think I'd be neah enough to see them."

"No," answered her father, "that is one of the sad facts of life. No matter how loudly we may cry for the moon, it is hung too high for us to reach, and the 'forget-me-nots of the angels,' as Longfellow calls the stars, are not for hands like ours to pick. But in a very little while I think that we shall see the lightning below us. Those clouds down there are full of rain. They may rise high enough to give us a wetting, so it would be wise for us to hurry back to the hotel."

"It is the strangest thing that evah happened to me in all my life!" said Lloyd a few minutes later, as they sat on the hotel piazza, watching the storm below them.   Overhead the summer sun was shining brightly, but just below the heavy storm clouds rolled, veiling all the valley from sight.   They could see the forked tongues of lightning darting back and forth far below them, and hear the heavy rumble of thunder.

"It seems so wondahful to think that we are safe up above the storm.   Look!   There is a rainbow! And there is anothah and anothah !   Oh, it is so beautiful, I'm glad it rained ! "

The storm, that had lasted for nearly an hour, gradually cleared away till the valley lay spread out before them once more, in the sunshine, green and dripping from the summer shower.

"Well," said the Little Colonel, as they started homeward, "aftah this I'll remembah that no mattah how hard it rains the sun is always shining somewhere.   It nevah hides itself from us.   It is the valley that gets behind the clouds, just as if it was puttin' a handkerchief ovah its face when it wanted to cry.   It's a comfort to know that the sun keeps shining, on right on, unchanged."

It was nearly dark when they reached the little inn again in Zug.   The narrow streets were wet, and the eaves of the houses still dripping.   The landlord came out to meet them with an anxious face.   "Your friend, the old Major," he said, in his broken English, "he have not yet return. I fear the storm for him was bad."

"Where did he go?" inquired Mr. Sherman. "I did not know that he intended leaving the hotel at all to-day. He did not seem well."

"Early after lunch," was the answer. "He say he will up the mountain go, behind the town. He say that now he vair old man, maybe not again will he come this way, and one more time already before he die, he long to gather for himself the Alpine rosen."

"Have you had a hard storm here?" asked Mrs. Sherman.

The landlord shrugged his shoulders and spread out his hands.

"The vair worst, madame. Many trees blow down. The lightning he strike a house next to the church of St. Oswald, and a goatherd coming down just now from the mountain say that the paths are heaped with fallen limbs, and slippery with mud. That is why for I fear the Major have one accident met."

"Maybe he has stopped at some peasant's hut for shelter," suggested Mr. Sherman, seeing the distress in Lloyd's face. "He knows the region around here thoroughly. However, if he is not here by the time we are through dinner, we'll organise a searching party."

"Hero knows that something is wrong," said the Little Colonel, as they went into the dining-room a few minutes later. "See how uneasy he seems, walking from room to room. He is trying to find his mastah."

The longer they discussed the Major's absence the more alarmed they became, as the time passed and he did not return.

"You know," suggested Lloyd, "that with just one arm he couldn't help himself much if he should fall. Maybe he has slipped down some of those muddy ravines that the goatherd told about. Besides, he was so weak and tiahed this mawnin.'"

Presently her face brightened with a sudden thought.

"Oh, Papa Jack! Let's send Hero. I know where the Majah keeps his things, the flask and the bags, and the dog will know, as soon as they are fastened on him, that he must start on a hunt. And I believe I can say the words in French so that he'll undahstand. Only yestahday the Majah had me repeating them."

"That's a bright idea," answered her father, who

"ALL THE GUESTS IN THE INN GATHERED AROUND THE
DOOR TO SEE HIM START"

was really more anxious than he allowed any one to
see. "At least it can do no harm to try."

"I don't want any dessert. Mayn't I go now?"
Lloyd asked. As she hurried up the stairs, her
heart beating with excitement, she whispered to
herself, "Oh, if he *should* happen to be lost or hurt,
and Hero should find him, it would be the loveliest
thing that evah happened."

Hero seemed to know, from the moment he saw
the little flask marked with the well-known Red
Cross, what was expected of him. All the guests in
the inn gathered around the door to see him start on
his uncertain quest. He sniffed excitedly at his
master's slipper, which Lloyd held out to him. Then,
as she motioned toward the mountain, and gave the
command in French that the Major had taught her,
he bounded out into the gloaming, with several quick
short barks, and darted up the narrow street that
led to the mountain road.

Maybe if he had not been with his master that
way, the day before, he might not have known what
path to take. The heavy rain had washed away all
trails, so he could not trace him by the sense of
smell; but remembering the path which they had
travelled together the previous day, he instinctively
started up that.

The group in the doorway of the inn watched him as long as they could see the white line of his silvery ruff gleam through the dusk, and then, going back to the parlour, sat down to wait for his return. To most of them it was a matter of only passing interest. They were curious to know how much the dog's training would benefit his master, under the circumstances, if he should be lost. But to the Little Colonel it seemed a matter of life and death. She walked nervously up and down the hall with her hands behind her, watching the clock and running to the door to peer out in the darkness, every time she heard a sound.

Some one played a noisy two-step on the loose-jointed old piano. A young man sang a serenade in Italian, and two girls, after much coaxing, consented to join in a high, shrill duet.

Light-hearted laughter and a babel of conversation floated from the parlour to the hall, where Lloyd watched and waited. Her father waited with her, but he had a newspaper. Lloyd wondered how he could read while such an important search was going on. She did not know that he had little faith in the dog's ability to find his master. She, however, had not a single doubt of it.

The time seemed endless. Again and again the

little cuckoo in the hall clock came out to call the hour, the quarters and halves. At last there was a patter of big soft paws on the porch, and Lloyd springing to the door, met Hero on the threshold. Something large and gray was in his mouth.

"Oh, Papa Jack!" she cried. "He's found him! Hero's found him! This is the Majah's Alpine hat. The flask is gone from his collah, so the Majah must have needed help. And see how wild Hero is to start back. Oh, Papa Jack! Hurry, please!"

Her call brought every one from the parlour to see the dog, who was springing back and forth with eager barks that asked, as plainly as words, for some one to follow him.

"Oh, let me go with you! *Please*, Papa Jack," begged Lloyd.

He shook his head decidedly. "No, it is too late and dark, and no telling how far we shall have to climb. You have already done your part, my dear, in sending the dog. If the Major is really in need of help, he will have you to thank for his rescue."

The landlord called for lanterns. Several of the guests seized their hats and alpenstocks, and in a few minutes the little relief party was hurrying along the street after their trusty guide, with Mr. Sherman in the lead. He had caught up a hammock as he started. "We may need some kind of a stretcher," he said, slinging it over his shoulder.

They trudged on in silence, wondering what they would find at the end of their journey. The mountain path was strewn with limbs broken off by the storm. Although the moon came up presently and added its faint light to the yellow rays of the lanterns, they had to pick their steps slowly, often stumbling.

Hero, bounding on ahead, paused to look back now and then, with impatient barks. They had climbed more than an hour, when he suddenly shot ahead into the darkest part of the woods and gave voice so loudly that they knew that they had reached the end of their search, and pushed forward anxiously.

The moonlight could not reach this spot among the trees, so densely shaded, but the lanterns showed them the old man a short distance from the path. He was pinned to the wet earth by a limb that had fallen partly across him. Fortunately, the storm had been unable to twist it entirely from the tree. Only the outer end of the limb had struck him, but the tangle of leafy boughs above him was too thick to creep through. His clothes were drenched, and on the ground beside him, beaten flat by the storm, lay the bunch of Alpine roses he had climbed so far to find.

He was conscious when the men reached him. The brandy in the flask had revived him and as they drew him out from under the branches and stretched the hammock over some poles for a litter, he told them what had happened. He had been some distance farther up the mountain, and had stopped at a peasant's hut for some goat's milk. He rested there a long time, never noticing in the dense shade of the woods that a storm was gathering.

It came upon him suddenly. His head was hurt, and his back. He could not tell how badly. He had lain so long on the wet ground that he was numb with cold, but thought he would be better when he was once more resting warm and dry at the inn.

He stretched out his hand to Hero and feebly patted him, a faint smile crossing his face. "Thou best of friends," he whispered. "Thou — " Then he stopped, closing his eyes with a groan. They were lifting him on the stretcher, and the pain caused by the movement made him faint.

It was a slow journey down the slippery mountain path. The men who carried him had to pick their steps carefully. At the inn the little cuckoo came out of the clock in the hall and called eleven, half past, and midnight, before the even tramp, tramp of approaching feet made the Little Colonel run to the door for the last time.

"They're comin', mothah," she whispered, with a frightened face, and then ran back to hide her eyes while the men passed up the steps with their unconscious burden.   She thought the Major was dead, he lay so white and still.   But he had only fainted again on the way, and soon revived enough to answer the doctor's questions, and send word to the Little Colonel that she and Hero had saved his life. "Do you heah that?" she asked of Hero, when they told her what he had said.   "The doctah said that if the Majah had lain out on that cold, wet ground till mawnin', without any attention, it surely would have killed him.   I'm proud of you, Hero. I'm goin' to get Papa Jack to write a piece about you and send it to the *Courier-Journal*.   How would you like to have yo' name come out in a big American newspapah?"

Several lonely days followed for the Little Colonel. Either her father or mother was constantly with the Major, and sometimes both.   They were waiting for his niece to come from Zürich and take him back with her to a hospital where he could have better care than in the little inn in Zug.

It greatly worried the old man that he should be the cause of disarranging their plans and delaying their journey. He urged them to go on and leave him, but they would not consent. Sometimes the Little Colonel slipped into the room with a bunch of Alpine roses or a cluster of edelweiss that she had bought from some peasant. Sometimes she sat beside him for a few minutes, but most of her time was spent with Hero, wandering up and down beside the lake, feeding the swans or watching the little steamboats come and go. She had forgotten her fear of the bottom dropping out of the town.

One evening, just at sunset, the Major sent for her. "I go to Zürich in the morning," he said, holding out his hand as she came into the room. "I wanted to say good-bye while I have the time and strength. We expect to leave very early to-morrow, probably before you are awake."

His couch was drawn up by the window, through which the shimmering lake shone in the sunset like rosy mother-of-pearl. Far up the mountain sounded the faint tinkling of goat-bells, and the clear, sweet yodelling of a peasant, on his homeward way. At intervals, the deep tolling of the bell of St. Oswald floated out across the water.

"When the snow falls," he said, after a long

pause, "I shall be far away from here. They tell me that at the hospital where I am going, I shall find a cure. But I know." He pointed to an hour-glass on the table beside him. "See! the sand has nearly run its course. The hour will soon be done. It is so with me. I have felt it for a long time."

Lloyd looked up, startled. He went on slowly.

"I cannot take Hero with me to the hospital, so I shall leave him behind with some one who will care for him and love him, perhaps even better than I have done." He held out his hand to the dog.

"Come, Hero, my dear old comrade, come bid thy master farewell." Fumbling under his pillow as he spoke, he took out a small leather case, and, opening it, held up a medal. It was the medal that had been given him for bravery on the field of battle.

"It is my one treasure!" murmured the old soldier, turning it fondly, as it lay in his palm. "I have no family to whom I can leave it as an heirloom, but thou hast twice earned the right to wear it. I have no fear but that thou wilt always be true to the Red Cross and thy name of Hero, so thou shalt wear thy country's medal to thy grave."

He fastened the medal to Hero's collar, then, with

the dog's great head pressed fondly against him, he began talking to him softly and gently in French. Lloyd could not understand, but the sight of the gray-haired old soldier taking his last leave of his faithful friend brought the tears to her eyes.

She tried to describe the scene to her mother, afterward.

"Oh, it was so pitiful!" she exclaimed. "It neahly broke my heart. Then he called me to him and said that because I was like his little Christine, he knew that I would be good to Hero, and he asked me to take him back to America with me. I promised that I would. Then he put Hero's paw in my hand, and said, 'Hero, I give thee to thy little mistress. Protect and guard her always, as she will love and care for thee.' It was awfully solemn, almost like some kind of blessing.

"Then he lay back on the pillows as if he was too tiahed to say anothah word. I tried to thank him, but I was so surprised and glad that Hero was mine, and yet so sorry to say good-bye to the Majah, that the right words wouldn't come. I just began to cry again. But I am suah the Majah undahstood. He patted my hand and smoothed my hair and said things in French that sounded as if he was tryin' to comfort me. Aftah awhile I remembahed that we had been there a long time, and ought to go, so I kissed him good-bye, and Hero and I went out, leavin' the doah open as he told us. He watched us all the way down the hall. When I turned at the stairway to look back, he was still watchin'. He smiled and waved his hand, but the way he smiled made me feel worse than evah, it was so sad."

Mr. Sherman went with the Major next morning, when he was taken to Zürich. Lloyd was asleep when they left the inn, so the last remembrance she had of the Major was the way he looked as he lay on his couch in the sunset, smiling, and waving his hand to her. When Christmastide came, it was as he said. He was with his little Christine.

"I can hardly keep from crying whenever I think of him," Lloyd wrote to Betty. "It was so pitiful, his giving up everything in the world that he cared for, and going off to the hospital to wait there alone for his hour-glass to run out. Hero seems to miss him, but I think he understands that he belongs to me now. I can scarcely believe that he is really mine, and that I may take him back to America with me. He is the best thing that the wonder-ball has given me, or ever can give me.

"To-morrow we start to Lucerne to see the Lion in the rocks, and from there we go to Paris. Only

a little while now, and we shall all be together. I
can hardly wait for you to see my lovely St. Bernard
with his Red Cross of Geneva, and the medal that he
has earned the right to wear."

CHAPTER VII.

IN TOURS

A DOZEN times between Paris and Tours the
Little Colonel turned from the car window to smile
at her mother, and say with a wriggle of impatience,
" Oh, I can't *wait* to get there! Won't Betty and
Eugenia be surprised to see us two whole days
earlier than they expected ! "

" But you mustn't count too much on seeing them
at the hotel the minute we arrive," her mother cau-
tioned her. " You know Cousin Carl wrote that
they were making excursions every day to the old
châteaux near there, and I think it quite probable
they will be away. So don't set your heart on seeing them before to-morrow night. Some of those
trips take two days."

Lloyd turned to the window again and tried to
busy herself with the scenes flying past: the peasant women with handkerchiefs over their heads, and
the men in blue cotton blouses and wooden shoes at
work in the fields; the lime-trees and the vineyards,

the milk-carts that dogs helped to draw. It was all as Joyce had described it to her, and she pinched herself to make sure that she was awake, and actually in France, speeding along toward the Gate of the Giant Scissors, and all the delightful foreign experience that Joyce had talked about. She had dreamed many day-dreams about this journey, but the thought that was giving her most pleasure now was not that these dreams were at last coming true, but that in a very short time she would be face to face with Betty and Eugenia.

It was noon when they reached Tours, and went rattling up to the Hotel Bordeaux in the big omnibus. At first Lloyd was disposed to find fault with the quaint, old-fashioned hotel which Cousin Carl had chosen as their meeting-place. It had no conveniences like the modern ones to which she had been accustomed. There was not even an elevator in it. She looked in dismay at the steep, spiral stairway, winding around and around in the end of the hall, like the steps in the tower of a lighthouse. On a side table in the hall, several long rows of candles, with snuffers, suggested the kind of light they would have in their bedrooms.

But everything was spotlessly clean, and the landlady and her daughter came out to meet them with an air of giving them a welcome home, which extended even to the dog. After their hospitable reception of Hero, Lloyd had no more fault to find. She knew that at no modern hotel would he have been treated so considerately and given the liberty of the house. Since he was not banished to the courtyard or turned over to a porter's care, she was willing to climb a dozen spiral stairways, or grope her way through the semi-darkness of a candle-lighted bedroom every night while they were in France, for the sake of having Hero free to come and go as he pleased.

"Come on!" she cried, gaily, to her mother, as a porter with a trunk on his shoulder led the way up the spiral stairs. "It makes me think of the old song you used to sing me about the spidah and the fly, 'The way into my pahlah is up a winding stair.' Nobody but a circus acrobat could run up the whole flight without getting dizzy. It's a good thing we are only goin' to the next floah."

She ran around several circles of steps, and then paused to look back at her mother, who was waiting for Mr. Sherman's helping arm. "The elephant now goes round and round when the band begins to play," quoted Lloyd, looking down on them, her face dimpling with laughter.

"Look out!" piped a shrill voice far above her. "I'm coming!" Lloyd gave a hasty glance upward to the top floor, and drew back against the wall. For down the banister, with the speed of a runaway engine, came sliding a small bare-legged boy. Around and around the dizzy spiral he went, hugging the railing closely, and bringing up with a tremendous bump against the newel post at the bottom.

"Hullo!" he said, coolly, looking up at the Little Colonel.

"It's *Henny!*" she exclaimed, in amazement. "Henderson Sattawhite! Of all people! How did you get heah?"

But the boy had no time to waste in talking. He stuck his thumb in his mouth, looked at her an instant, and then, climbing down from the banister, started to the top of the stairs as fast as his short legs could carry him, for another downward spin.

Lloyd waited for her mother to come up to the step on which she stood, and then said, with a look of concern, "Do you suppose they are all heah, 'Fido' an' all of them? And that Howl will follow me around as he did on shipboard, beggin' for stories? It will spoil all my fun with the girls if he does."

"'Never trouble trouble till trouble troubles you,'"

said her father, playfully pinching her cheek. "You'll find it easier to escape persecution on land than or shipboard. Henny didn't seem at all anxious to renew his acquaintance with you. He evidently finds sliding down bannisters more to his taste. Maybe Howell has found something equally interesting."

"I certainly hope so," said Lloyd, running on to their rooms at the end of the hall. The casement window in her room looked out over a broad boulevard, down the middle of which went a double row of trees, shading a strip of grass, where benches were set at intervals.

Lloyd leaned out to look and listen. A company of soldiers was marching up the street in the gay red and blue of their French uniforms, to the music of a band. A group of girls from a convent school passed by. Then some nuns. She stood there a long time, finding the panorama that passed her window so interesting that she forgot how time was passing, until her mother called to her that they were going down to lunch.

"I like it heah, evah so much," she announced, as she followed her father and mother into the diningroom. "Did you ask in the office, Papa Jack, when the girls would be back?"

"Yes, they have gone to Amboise. They will be

home before dark. I am sorry you missed taking
that trip with them, Lloyd. It is one of the most
interesting châteaux around here in my opinion.
Mary, Queen of Scots, went there a bride. There
she was forced to watch the Hugenots being thrown
over into the river. Leonardo da Vinci is buried
there, and Charles VIII. was killed there by bumping his head against a low doorway."

" Oh, deah ! " sighed the Little Colonel, " my head
is all in a tangle. There's so many spots to remembah. Every time you turn around you bump
into something you ought to remembah because
some great man was bawn there, or died there, or
did something wondahful there. It would be lots
easiah for travellers in Europe if there wasn't so
many monuments to smaht people. Who must I
remembah in Tours?"

"Balzac," said her father, laughing. "The great
French novelist. But that will not be hard. There
is a statue of him on one of the principal streets,
and after you have passed him every day for a week,
you will think of him as an old acquaintance. Then
this is the scene of one of Scott's novels — ' Quentin
Durward.' And the good St. Martin lived here.
There is a church to his memory. He is the patron
saint of the place. At the châteaux you will get into

a tangle of history, for their chief interest is their associations with the old court life."

"Where is Hero?" asked Mrs. Sherman, suddenly changing the conversation.

"He's in the pahlah, stretched out on a rug," answered Lloyd. "It's cool and quiet in there with the blinds down. The landlady's daughtah said no one went in there often, in the middle of the day, so nobody would disturb him, and he'd not disturb anybody. He's all tiahed out, comin' so far on the cars. May I go walkin' with him aftah awhile, mothah?"

Mrs. Sherman looked at her husband, questioningly. "Oh, it's perfectly safe," he answered. "She could go alone here as well as in Lloydsboro Valley, and with Hero she could have nothing to fear."

"I want you to rest awhile first," said Mrs. Sherman. "At four o'clock you may go."

Leaving Hero comfortably stretched out asleep in the parlour, Lloyd went back to her room. She lay down for a few minutes across the bed and closed her eyes. But she could not sleep with so many interesting sights in the street below. Presently she tiptoed to the window, and sat looking out until she heard her mother moving around in the next room. She knew then that she had had her nap and was unpacking the trunks.

"Mothah," called Lloyd, "I want to put on my prettiest white embroidered dress and my rosebud sash, because I'll meet Cousin Carl and the girls to-night."

"That is just what I have unpacked for you," said her mother. "Come in and I'll help you dress."

Half an hour later it was a very fresh and dainty picture that smiled back at Lloyd from the mirror of her dressing-table. She shook out her crisp white skirts, gave the rosebud sash an admiring pat, and turned her head for another view of the big leghorn hat with its stylish rosettes of white chiffon. Then she started down the hall toward the spiral stairway. It was a narrow hall with several cross passages, and at one of them she paused, wondering if it did not lead to Eugenia's and Betty's rooms.

To her speechless surprise, a door popped open and a cupful of water was dashed full in her face. Spluttering and angry, she drew back in time to avoid another cupful, which came flying through the transom above the same door. Retreating still farther down the passage, and wiping her face as she went, she kept her gaze on the door, walking backward in order to do so.

Another cupful came splashing out into the hall through the transom. A boy, tiptoeing up to the door, dodged back so quickly that not a drop touched him ; then with a long squirt gun that he carried, he knelt before the keyhole and sent a stream of water squirting through it. It was Howell.

There was a scream from the bedroom, Fidelia's voice. "Stop that, you hateful boy! I'll tell mamma! You've nearly put my eye out."

A muffled giggle and a scamper of feet down the hall was the only answer. Fidelia threw open the door and looked out, a water pitcher in her hand. She stopped in amazement at sight of the Little Colonel, who was waiting for a chance to dodge down the hall past the dangerous door, into the main passage.

"For mercy sakes!" exclaimed Fidelia. "When did *you* come?"

"In time fo' yoah watah fight," answered the indignant Little Colonel, shaking out her wet handkerchief. She was thoroughly provoked, for the front of her fresh white dress was drenched, and the dainty rosebud sash streaked with water.

"HE KNELT BEFORE THE KEYHOLE AND SENT A STREAM
OF WATER SQUIRTING THROUGH IT"

Fidelia laughed. "You don't mean to say that you caught the ducking I meant for Howl!" she exclaimed. "Well, if that isn't a joke! It's the funniest thing I ever heard of!" Putting the pitcher on the floor and clasping her hands to her sides, she laughed until she had to lean against the wall.

"It's moah bad mannahs than a joke!" retorted Lloyd, angered more by the laugh than she had been by the wetting. "A girl as old as you oughtn't to go travellin' till you know how to behave yo'self in a hotel. I don't wondah that wherevah you go people say, 'Oh, those dreadful American children!'"

"It isn't so! They don't say it!" snapped Fidelia. "I've got just as good manners as you have, anyhow, and I'll throw this whole pitcher of water on you if you say another word." She caught it up threateningly.

"You just *dare!*" cried the Little Colonel, her eyes flashing and her cheeks flushing. Not for years had she been so angry. She wanted to scream and pull Fidelia's hair with savage fingers. She wanted to bump her head against the wall, again and again. But with an effort so great that it made her tremble, she controlled herself, and stood looking steadily at Fidelia without a word.

"I mustn't speak," she kept saying desperately to

herself. "I mustn't speak, or my tempah will get away with me. I might claw her eyes out. I wish I could! Oh, I *wish* I could!" Her teeth were set tightly together, and her hands were clenched.

Fidelia met her angry gaze unflinchingly for an instant, and then, with a contemptuous "pooh!" raised the pitcher and gave it a lurch forward. It was so heavy that it turned in her hands, and instead of drenching Lloyd, its contents deluged Fanchette, who suddenly came out of the door beside Lloyd, with the thousand dollar poodle in her arms.

Poor Beauty gave an injured yelp, and Fidelia drew back and slammed the door, locking it hastily. She knew that the maid would hurry to her mistress while he was still shivering, and that there would be an uncomfortable account to settle by and by.

Howell, who had crept up to watch the fuss, doubled himself with laughter. It amused him even more than it had Fidelia that he had escaped the water, and Lloyd had caught it in his stead. Lloyd swept past him without a word, and ran to her mother's room so angry that she could not keep the tears back while telling her grievance.

" *See* what that horrid Sattawhite girl has done!" she cried, holding out her limp wet skirts, and streaked sash, with an expression of disgust. I just *despise* her!"

"It was an accident, was it not?" asked Mrs. Sherman.

"Oh, she didn't know she was throwing the watah on me, when she pitched it out, but she was glad that it happened to hit me. She didn't even say 'excuse me,' let alone say that she was sorry. And she laughed and held on to her sides, and laughed again, and said, 'oh, what a joke,' and that it was the funniest thing that she evah saw. I think her mothah ought to know what bad mannahs she's got. Somebody ought to tell her. I told Fidelia what I thought of her, and I'll nevah speak to her again! So there!"

Mrs. Sherman listened sympathetically to her tale of woe, but as she unbuttoned the wet dress, and Lloyd still stormed on, she sighed as if to herself, "Poor Fidelia!"

"Why, mothah," said Lloyd, in an aggrieved tone, "I didn't s'pose that you'd take her part against me."

"Stop and think a minute, little daughter," said Mrs. Sherman, opening her trunk to take out another white dress. Lloyd was working herself up into a white heat. "Put yourself in Fidelia's place, and think how she has always been left to the care of

servants, or of a governess who neglected her. Think
how much help you have had in trying to control
your temper, and how little you have had to provoke
it. Suppose you had Howell and Henderson always
tagging after you to tease and annoy you, and that I
had always been too busy with my own affairs to
take any interest in you, except to punish you when
I was exasperated by the tales that you told of each
other. Wouldn't that have made a difference in
your manners?"

"Y-yes," acknowledged Lloyd, slowly. Then, after
a moment's silence, she broke out again. "I might
have forgiven her if only she hadn't laughed at me.
Whenevah I think of that I want to shake her. If
I live to be a hundred yeahs old, I can nevah think
of Fidelia Sattawhite, without remembahin' the mean
little way she laughed!"

"What kind of a memory are you leaving behind
you?" suggested Mrs. Sherman, touching the little
ring on Lloyd's finger that had been her talisman
since the house party. "Will it be a Road of the
Loving Heart?"

Lloyd hesitated. "No," she acknowledged, frankly.
"Of co'se when I stop to think, I do want to leave
that kind of a memory for everybody. I'd hate to
think that when I died, there'd be even one person

who had cause to say ugly things about me, even Fidelia. But just now, mothah, honestly when I remembah how she *laughed*, I feel that I must be as mean to her as she is to me. I can't help it."

Mrs. Sherman made no answer, but turned to her own dressing, and presently Lloyd kissed her, and went slowly down-stairs to find Hero. He was no longer dreaming in peace. Two restless boys cooped up in the narrow limits of the hotel, and burning with a desire to be amused, had discovered him through the crack of the door, and immediately pounced upon him.

"Aw, ain't he nice!" exclaimed Henny, stroking the shaggy back with a dirty little hand. Howl felt in his blouse, hoping to find some crumb left of the stock of provisions stored away at lunch-time.

"Feel there, Henny," he commanded, backing up to his little brother, and humping his shoulders. "Ain't that a cooky slipped around to the back of my blouse? Put your hand up and feel."

Henny obligingly explored the back of his brother's blouse, and fished out the last cooky, which they fed to Hero.

"Wisht we had some more," said Howell, as the cake disappeared. "Henny, you go up and see if you can't hook some of Beauty's biscuit."

"Naw! I don't want to. I want to play with the dog," answered Henny. "He's big enough to ride on. Stand up, old fellow, and let me get on your back."

"I'll tell you a scheme," cried Howl; "you run up-stairs and get one of mamma's shawl-straps, and we'll fix a harness for him, and make him ride us around the room."

"All right," agreed Henny, trotting out into the hall. At the door he met Lloyd. When she went into the room she found Howell lying on the floor, burrowing his head into the dog's side for a pillow. Hero did not like it, and, shaking himself free, walked across the room and lay down in another place.

Howl promptly followed, and pillowed his head on him again. Hero looked around with an appealing expression in his big, patient eyes, once more got up, crossed the room, and lay down in a corner. Howell followed him like a teasing mosquito.

"Don't bothah him, Howl," said Lloyd. "Don't you see that he doesn't like it?"

"But he makes such a nice, soft pillow," said the boy, once more burrowing his hard little head into Hero's ribs.

"He might snap at you if you tease him too

much. I nevah saw him do it to any one, but
nobody has evah teased him since he belonged to
me."

"Is he your dog?" asked Howl, in surprise.

"Yes," answered Lloyd, proudly. "He saved my
life one time, and his mastah's anothah. And that
medal on his collah was one that was given by France
to his mastah fo' bravery, and the Majah gave it to
him because he said that Hero had twice earned the
right to wear it."

"Tell about it," demanded Howl, scenting a story.
"How did he —" His question was stopped in the
middle by Hero, who, determined to be no longer
used as a pillow, stood up and gave himself a mighty
shake. Walking over to the sofa piled with cushions, he took one in his mouth, and carrying it back
to Howl dropped it at his feet as if to say, "There!
Use that! I am no sofa pillow." That done he
stretched himself out again in the farthest corner of
the room, and laid his head on his paws with a sigh
of relief.

"Oh! Oh!" cried the Little Colonel. "Did you
evah see anything so sma'ht as that in all yo' life?
It's the brightest thing I evah saw a dog do. He
thought it all out, just like a person. I wish Papa
Jack could have seen him do it. I'm goin' to treat

you to something nice fo' that, Hero. Wait till I run back up-stairs and get my purse."

Anxious to make him do something else interesting, Howl still followed the dog. He tickled his paws, turned his ears back and blew in them and blindfolded him with a dirty handkerchief.

Lloyd was gone longer than she intended, for she could not find her purse for several minutes, and she stopped to tell her mother of Hero's performance with the sofa pillow. When she went into the parlour again, both boys were kneeling beside the dog. Their backs were toward the door, Henderson had brought the shawl-strap, and they were using it for the further discomfort of the patient old St. Bernard.

"Here, Henny, you sit on his head," commanded Howl, "and I'll buckle his hind feet to his fore feet, so that when he tries to walk he'll wabble around and tip over. Won't that be funny?"

"Stop!" demanded Lloyd. "Don't you do that, Howl Sattawhite! I've told you enough times to stop teasing my dog."

Howl only giggled in reply and drew the buckle tighter. There was a quick yelp of pain, and Hero, trying to pull away, found himself fast by the foot.

Before Howl could rise from his knees, the Little Colonel had darted across the room, and seizing him by the shoulders, shook him till his teeth chattered.

" There ! " she said, giving him a final shake as she pushed him away. " Don't you evah lay a fingah on that dog again, as long as you live. If you do you'll be sorry. I'll do something *awful* to you ! "

For the second time that afternoon her face was white with anger. Her eyes flashed so threateningly that Howl backed up against the wall, thoroughly frightened. Releasing Hero from the strap, she led him out of the room, and, with her hand laid protectingly on his collar, marched him out into the street.

" Those tawmentin' Sattawhites ! " she grumbled, under her breath. " I wish they were all shut up in jail, every one of them ! "

But her anger died out as she walked on in the bright sunshine, watching the strange scenes around her with eager eyes. More than one head turned admiringly, as the daintily dressed little girl and the great St. Bernard passed slowly down the broad boulevard. It seemed as if all the nurses and babies in Touraine were out for an airing on the grass where the benches stood, between the long double rows of trees.

Once Lloyd stopped to peep through a doorway

set in a high stone wall. Within the enclosure a group of girls, in the dark uniforms of a charity school, walked sedately around, arm in arm, under the watchful eyes of the attendant nuns. Then some soldiers passed on foot, and a little while after, some more dashed by on horseback, and she remembered that Tours was the headquarters of the Ninth Army corps, and that she might expect to meet them often.

Not till the tolling of the great cathedral bell reminded her that it was time to go back to the hotel, did she think again of Howl and Henny and Fidelia. By that time her walk had put her into such a pleasant frame of mind, that she could think of them without annoyance.

CHAPTER VIII.

WITH BETTY AND EUGENIA

When the Little Colonel reached the hotel, the omnibus was leaving the door to go to the railroad station, a few blocks away. Thinking that Betty and Eugenia might be on the coming train, she went into the parlour to wait for the return of the omnibus. She had bought a box of chocolate creams at the cake shop on the corner to divide with Hero.

Fidelia had wandered down to the parlour in her absence, and now seated at the old piano was banging on its yellow keys with all her might. She played unusually well for a girl of her age, but Lloyd had a feeling that a public parlour was not a place to show off one's accomplishments, and her nose went up a trifle scornfully as she entered.

Then she caught sight of herself in the mirror over the mantel, and her expression changed instantly.

"For mercy sakes!" she said to herself. "I

look like one of the proud and haughty sistahs in 'Cindahella,' as if I thought the earth wasn't good enough for me to step on. It certainly isn't becoming, and it would make me furious if anybody looked at me in such a cool, scornful way. I know that I feel that way inside whenevah I talk to Fidelia. I wondah if she sees it in my face, and that's what makes her cross and scratchy, like a cat that has had its fur rubbed the wrong way. Just for fun I believe I'll pretend to myself for ten minutes that I love her deahly, and I'll smile when I talk to her, just as if she were Betty, and nevah pay any attention to her mean speeches. I'll give her this one chance. Then if she keeps on bein' hateful, I'll nevah have anything moah to do with her again."

So while Fidelia played on toward the end of the waltz, purposely regardless of Lloyd's presence, Lloyd, sitting behind her, looked into the mirror, and practised making pleasant faces for Fidelia's benefit.

The music came to a close with a loud double bang that made Lloyd start up from her chair with a guilty flush, fearing that she had been caught at her peculiar occupation. Before Fidelia could say anything, Lloyd walked over to her with the friendliest of her practised smiles, and held out the box of chocolate creams.

"Take some," she said. "They are the best I've had since I left Kentucky."

"Thanks," said Fidelia, stiffly, screwing around on the piano-stool, and helping herself to just one. But feeling the warmth of Lloyd's cordial tone, urging her to take more, she thawed into smiling friendliness, and took several. "They are delicious!" she exclaimed. "You got them at the cake shop on the corner, didn't you? There are two awfully nice American girls stopping at this hotel who took me in there one day for some. They've been in Kentucky, too. The one named Elizabeth lives there."

"Why, it must be Betty and Eugenia!" cried Lloyd. "The very girls we came here to meet. Do *you* know them?"

"Not very well. We've only been here a few days. But I dearly love the one you call Betty. She came into my room one night when I had the tooth-ache, and brought a spice poultice and a hot-water bag. Mamma was at a concert, and Fanchette was cross, and I was so miserable and lonesome I wanted to die. But Elizabeth knew exactly what to do to stop the pain, and then she stayed and talked to me for a long time. She told me about a house party she went to last year, where the girls all caught the measles at a gypsy camp, and she nearly went blind on account of it."

"That was *my* house pahty," exclaimed the Little Colonel, "and my mothah is Betty's godmothah, and Betty is goin' to live at my house all next wintah, and go to school with me."

Fidelia swung farther around on the piano-stool, and faced Lloyd in surprise. "And are *you* the Little Colonel!" she cried. "From what Elizabeth said, I thought she was pretty near an angel!" Fidelia's tone implied more plainly than her words that she wondered how Betty could think so.

A cutting reply was on the tip of Lloyd's tongue, but the sight of her face in the mirror checked it. She only said, pleasantly, "Betty is certainly the loveliest girl in the world, and —"

"There she is now!" interrupted Fidelia, nodding toward the door as voices sounded in the hall and footsteps came out from the office.

"Oh, they'll be so surprised!" said Lloyd, looking back with a radiant face as she ran toward the door. "We came two whole days earlier than they expected!"

Fidelia heard the joyful greeting, the chorus of surprised exclamations as Lloyd flew first at Betty, then at Eugenia, with a hug and a kiss, then turned to greet her Cousin Carl.

"Betty will never look at me again," Fidelia thought, with a throb of jealousy, turning away from the sight of their happy meeting, and beginning to strike soft aimless chords on the piano. "I wish I were one of them," she whispered, with the tears springing to her eyes. "I hate to be always on the edge of things, and never in them. We never stay in a place long enough at a time to make any real friends or have any good times."

Chattering and laughing, and asking eager questions, the girls hurried up the stairs to Mrs. Sherman's room. Almost a year had gone by since Eugenia and Lloyd had parted on the lantern decked lawn at Locust, the last night of the house party. The year had made little difference in Lloyd, but Eugenia had grown so tall that the change was startling.

"Really, you are taller than I," exclaimed Mrs. Sherman, in the midst of an affectionate greeting, as she held her off for a better view.

"And doesn't she look stylish and young ladyfied, with her skirts down to her ankles," added Lloyd. "You'd nevah think that she was only fifteen, would you?"

"I had to have them made long," explained Eugenia, much flattered by Lloyd's speech. It was her greatest wish to appear "grown up." "Papa says that I am probably as tall now as I shall ever be, and really I'd look ridiculous with my dresses any shorter."

Mrs. Sherman noticed presently, with a smile, that Eugenia seemed to have gained dignity with her added height. There was something amusingly patronising in her manner toward the younger girls. She answered Lloyd several times with an "Oh, no, child" that was almost grandmotherly in its tone.

"But here is somebody who has come back just as sweet and childlike as ever," thought Mrs. Sherman, twisting one of Betty's brown curls around her finger. Then she said aloud. "Was the trip as delightful as you dreamed it would be, my little Tusitala?"

"Oh, *yes*, godmother," sighed Betty, blissfully. "It was a thousand times better! And the best of it is my eyes are as well as ever. I needn't be afraid, now, of that 'long night' that haunted me like a bad dream."

All during dinner Fidelia kept looking across at the merry party sitting at the next table, and wished she could be with them. She could not help hearing all they said, for they were only a few feet away, and there was no one talking at the table where she sat. The boys were in the children's dining-room with Fanchette, and her mother was spending the evening with some friends at the new hotel across the way.

"I'm going to make believe that I'm one of them," the lonely child said to herself, smiling as she caught a friendly nod from Betty. So she listened eagerly to Mr. Forbes's account of their visit to Venice, and to the volcano of Vesuvius, and laughed with the others over the amusing experiences Betty and Eugenia had in Norway with a chambermaid who could not understand them, and in Holland with an old Dutch market-woman, the day they became separated from Mr. Forbes, and were lost for several hours.

Fidelia's salad almost choked her, there was such an ache in her throat when she heard them planning an excursion for the next day. She had no one to make plans with, and when she was taken sightseeing it was by a French teacher, more intent on improving her pupil's accent than in giving her a happy time.

As they were finishing their dessert, Mr. Sherman suddenly remembered that he had a letter in his pocket for Lloyd, which he had forgotten to give her.

"It is from Joyce," she said, looking at the post-mark. "Oh, if she were only heah, what a lovely time we could have! It would be like havin' anothah house pahty. May I read it now at the table, mothah? It is to all of us."

Fidelia almost held her breath. She was so afraid that Mrs. Sherman would suggest waiting until they went to the parlour. There she could no longer be one of them, no matter how hard she might pretend. She wanted the interesting play to go on as long as possible. She did not know that she ought not to listen. There were many things she had never been taught. Lloyd began to read aloud.

"Dear Girls:— You will be in Tours by the time this letter reaches you, and I am simply wild to be there with you. Oh, if I could be there only one day to take you to all the old places! Do please go to the home of the 'Little Sisters of the Poor,' and ask for Sister Denisa. Give her my love, and tell her that I often think of her. And do go to that funny pie shop on the Rue Nationale, where everybody is allowed to walk around and help themselves and keep their own count. And eat one of those tiny delicious tarts for me. They're the best in the world.

"I can't think of anything else to-day, but that

walk which you will be taking soon without me. I can shut my eyes and see every inch of the way, as it used to look when we went home just after sunset. There is the river Loire all rosy red in the afterglow, and the bridge with the soldiers marching across it; and on the other side of the river is the little old village of St. Symphorian with its narrow, crooked streets. How I love every old cobblestone! You will see the fat old women rattling home in their market carts, and hear the clang and click of wooden shoes down the streets. Then there'll be the high gate of customs in the old stone wall that fences in the village, and the country road beyond. You'll climb the hill with the new moon coming up behind the tall Lombardy poplars, and go on between the fields, turning brown in the twilight, till the Gate of the Giant Scissors looms up beside the road like a picture out of some fairy tale. A little farther on you'll come to Madame's dear old villa with the high wall around it, and the laurel hedges and lime-trees inside.

"I wonder which of you will have my room with the blue parrots on the wall-paper. Oh, I'm *home-sick* to go back. Yet, isn't it strange, when I was there I used to long so for America, that many a time I climbed up in the pear-tree at the end of the

garden for a good cry.   Don't forget to swing up
into that pear-tree.   There's a fine view from the top.

"When you see Jules, ask him to show you the
goats that chewed up the cushions of the pony cart,
the day we had our Thanksgiving barbecue in the
garden.   I fairly ache to be with you.   Please write
me a good long letter and tell me what you are doing;
and whenever you hear the nightingales in Madame's
garden, and the cathedral bells tolling out across the
Loire, think of your loving   JOYCE."

"Let's do those things to-morrow," exclaimed
Lloyd, as she folded the letter and slipped it back
into its envelope.   "I don't want to waste time on
any old châteaux with the Gate of the Giant Scissors
just across the river, that we haven't seen yet."

"I have heard about that gate ever since we left
America," said Mr. Forbes, laughingly.   "Nobody
has taken the trouble to inform me why it is so
important, or why it was selected for a meeting-place.
Somebody owes me an explanation."

"It's only an old gate with a mammoth pair of
scissors swung on a medallion above it," said Mr.
Sherman.   "They were put there by a half-crazy old
man who built the place, by the name of *Ciseaux*.
Joyce Ware spent a winter in sight of it, and she

came back with some wonderful tale about the scissors being the property of a prince who went around doing all sorts of impossible things with them. I believe the girls have actually come to think that the scissors are enchanted."

"Oh, Papa Jack, stop teasin'!" said the Little Colonel. "You know we don't!"

"If it is really settled that we are to go there to-morrow, I want to hear the story," said Cousin Carl. "I make a practice of reading the history of a place before I visit it, so I'll have to know the story of the gate in order to take a proper interest in it."

"Come into the parlour," said Mrs. Sherman, rising. "Betty will tell us."

As she turned, she saw Fidelia looking after the girls with wistful eyes, and she read the longing and loneliness in her face.

"Wouldn't you like to come too, and hear the fairy tale with us?" she asked, kindly holding out her hand.

A look of happy surprise came over Fidelia's face, and before she could stammer out her acceptance of the unlooked-for invitation, Mrs. Sherman drew her toward her and led her into the little circle in one corner of the parlour.

"Now, we are ready, Tusitala," said Mrs. Sherman, settling herself on the sofa, with Fidelia beside her.   Shaking back her brown curls, Betty began the fairy tale that Joyce's Cousin Kate had told one bleak November day, to make the homesick child forget that she was "a stranger in a strange land."

"Once upon a time, in a far island of the sea, there lived a king with seven sons."

Word for word as she had heard it, Betty told the adventures of the princes ("the three that were dark and the three that were fair"), and then of the middle son, Prince Ethelried, to whom the old king gave no portion of his kingdom.   With no sword, nothing but the scissors of the Court Tailor, he had been sent out into the world to make his fortune. Even Cousin Carl listened with close attention to the prince's adventures with the Ogre, in which he was victorious, because the grateful fairy whom he had rescued laid on the scissors a magic spell.

" Here," she said, giving them into his hands again, " because thou wast persevering and fearless in setting me free, these shall win for thee thy heart's desire.   But remember that thou canst not keep them sharp and shining unless they are used at least once each day in some unselfish service."   After that he had only to utter his request in rhyme, and immediately they would shoot out to an enormous size that could cut down forests for him, bridge chasms, and reap whole wheat fields at a single stroke.

Many a peasant he befriended, shepherds and high-born dames, lords and lowly beggars ; and at the last, when he stood up before the Ogre to fight for the beautiful princess kept captive in the tower, it was their voices, shouting out their tale of gratitude to him for all these unselfish services, that made the scissors grow long enough and strong enough to cut the ugly old Ogre's head off.

"So he married the princess," concluded Betty at last, "and came into the kingdom that was his heart's desire. There was feasting and merrymaking for seventy days and seventy nights, and they all lived happily ever after. On each gable of the house he fastened a pair of shining scissors to remind himself that only through unselfish service to others comes the happiness that is highest and best. Over the great entrance gate he hung the ones that served him so valiantly, saying, 'Only those who belong to the kingdom of loving hearts can ever enter here'; and to this day they guard the portal of Ethelried, and only those who belong to the kingdom of loving hearts may enter the Gate of the Giant Scissors."

"Go on," said Mr. Forbes, as Betty stopped. "What happened next? I want to hear some more."

"So did Joyce," said Betty. "She used to climb up in the pear-tree and watch the gate, wishing she knew what lay behind it, and one day she found out. A poor little boy lived there with only the care-taker and another servant. The care-taker beat him and half starved him. His uncle didn't know how he was treated, for he was away in Algiers. Joyce found this little Jules out in the fields one day, tending the goats, and they got to be great friends. She told him this story, and they played that he was the prince and she was the Giant Scissors who was to rescue him from the clutches of the Ogre. She made up a rhyme for him to say. He had only to whisper :

"' Giant Scissors, fearless friend,
     Hasten, pray, thy aid to lend,'

and she would fly to help him. She really did, too, for she played ghost one night to frighten the old care-taker, and she told Jules's uncle, when he came back, how cruelly the poor little thing had been treated.

"Then the little prince really did come into his kingdom, for all sorts of lovely things happened after that. The gate had been closed for years on account of a terrible quarrel in the Ciseaux family, but at last something Joyce did helped to make it up. The gate swung open, and the old white-haired brother and sister went back to the home of their childhood together, and it was Christmas Day in the morning. They had been kept from going through the gate all those years, because the Giant Scissors wouldn't let them pass. Only those who belong to the kingdom of loving hearts can enter in."

"Some day you must put that all in a book, Betty," said Cousin Carl, when she had finished. "When we go to see the gate, I'll take my camera, and we'll get a picture of it. Now I feel that I can properly appreciate it, having heard its wonderful history."

There was a teasing light in his eyes that made Lloyd say, "Now you're laughin' at us, Cousin Carl, but it doesn't make any difference. I'd rathah see that gate than any old château in France."

CHAPTER IX.

AT THE GATE OF THE GIANT SCISSORS

EACH of the girls answered Joyce's letter, but the Little Colonel's was the first to find its way to the little brown house in Plainsville, Kansas.

"Dear Joyce," she wrote. "We were all dreadfully disappointed yesterday morning when mother and Papa Jack came back from Madame's villa, and told us that she could not let us stay there. She has some English people in the house, and could not give us rooms even for one night. She said that we must be disappointed also about seeing Jules, for his Uncle Martin has taken him to Paris to stay a month. I could have cried, I was so sorry.

"Ever since we left home I have been planning what we should do when we reached the Gate of the Giant Scissors. I wanted to do all the things that you did, as far as possible. I was going to have a barbecue for Jules, down in the garden by the pagoda, and to have some kind of a midsummer fête for the peasant children who came to your Christmas tree.

"Madame was sorry, too, that she couldn't take us, when she found that we were your friends, and she asked mother to bring us all out the next day and have tea in the pagoda. As soon as mother and Papa Jack came back, they took us to see Sister Denisa at the home of the Little Sisters of the Poor. I wish you could have seen her face shine when we told her that we were friends of yours. She said lovely things about you, and the tears came into her eyes when she told us how much she missed your visits, after you went back to America.

"Next day we went to Madame's, and she took us over to the Ciseaux place to see Jules's great-aunt Désirée. She is a beautiful old lady. She talked about you as if you were an angel, or a saint with a halo around your head. She feels that if it hadn't been for you that she might still be only 'Number Thirty-nine' among all those paupers, instead of being the mistress of her brother's comfortable home.

"After we left there, we passed the place where Madame's washerwoman lives. A little girl peeped out at us through the hedge. Madame told her to show the American ladies the doll that she had in her arms. She held it out, and then snatched it back as if she were jealous of our even looking at it. Madame told us that it was the one you gave her at the Noel fête. It is the only doll the child ever had, and she has carried it ever since, even taking it to bed with her. She has named it for you.

"Madame said in her funny broken English, 'Ah, it is a beautiful thing to leave such memories behind one as Mademoiselle Joyce has left.' I would have told her about the Road of the Loving Heart, but it is so hard for her to understand anything I say. I think you began yours over here in France, long before Betty told us of the one in Samoa, or Eugenia gave us the rings to help us remember.

"We took Fidelia Sattawhite with us. She is the girl I wrote to you about who was so rude to me, and who quarrelled so much with her brothers on shipboard. I thought it would spoil everything to have her along, but mother insisted on my inviting her. She feels sorry for her. Fidelia acted very well until we went over to the Ciseaux place. But when we got to the gate she stood and looked up at the scissors over it, and refused to go in. Madame and mother both coaxed and coaxed her, but she was too queer for anything. She wouldn't move a step. She just stood there in the road, saying, 'No'm, I won't go in. I don't want to. I'll stay out here and wait for you. No'm, nothing anybody can say can make me go in.'

"Down she sat on the grass as flat as Humpty Dumpty when he had his great fall, and all the king's horses and all the king's men couldn't have made her get up till she was ready. We couldn't understand why she should act so. She told Betty that night that she was afraid to go through the gate. She remembered that in the story where the old king and the brothers of Ethelried came riding up to the portal 'the scissors leaped from their place and snapped so angrily in their faces that they turned and fled. Only those who belong to the king-dom of loving hearts could enter in.' She told Betty that she knew she didn't belong to that kingdom, for nobody loved her, and often she didn't love anybody for days. She was afraid to go through the gate for fear the scissors would leap down at her, and she would be so ashamed to be driven back before us all. So she thought she would pretend that she didn't want to go in. She had believed every word of that fairy tale.

"We had a beautiful time in the garden. We went down all the winding paths between the high laurel hedges where you used to walk, and almost got lost, they had so many unexpected twists and turns.

The old statues of Adam and Eve, grinning at each other across the fountain, are so funny. We saw the salad beds with the great glass bells over them, and we climbed into the pear-tree and sat looking over the wall, wondering how you could have been homesick in such an interesting place.

" Berthé served tea in the pagoda, and because we asked about Gabriel's music, Madame smiled and sent Berthé away with a message. Pretty soon we heard his old accordeon playing away, out of sight in the coach-house, and then we knew what kind of music you had at the Noel fête. Sort of wheezy, wasn't it? Still it sounded sweet, too, at that distance.

" We took Hero with us, and he was really the guest of honour at the party. When Madame saw the Red Cross on his collar and heard his history, she couldn't do enough for him. She fed him cakes until I thought he surely would be ill. It was a Red Cross nurse who wrote to Madame about her husband. He was wounded in the Franco-Prussian war, too, just as was the Major. Madame went on to get him and bring him home, and she says she never can forget the kindness that was shown to her by every one whom she met when she crossed the lines under the protection of the Red Cross.

"She had met Clara Barton, too, and while we were talking about the good she has done, Madame said, 'The Duchess of Baden may have sent her the Gold Cross of Remembrance, but the grateful hearts of many a French wife and mother will for ever hold the rosary of her beautiful deeds!' Wasn't that a lovely thing to have said about one?

"We start to London Thursday, and I'll write again from there. With much love from us all, Lloyd."

The long letter which Lloyd folded and addressed after a careful re-reading, had not been all written in one day. She had begun it while waiting for the others to finish dressing one morning, had added a few pages that afternoon, and finished it the next evening at bedtime.

"Heah is my lettah to Joyce, mothah," she said, as she kissed her good night. "Won't you look ovah it, please, and see if all the words are spelled right? I want to send it in the mawnin."

Mrs. Sherman laid the letter aside to attend to later, and forgot it until long after Lloyd was asleep, and Mr. Sherman had come up-stairs. Then, seeing it on the table, she glanced rapidly over the neatly written pages.

"I want you to look at this, Jack," she said, presently, handing him the letter. "It is one of the results of the house party for which I am most thankful. You remember what a task it always was for Lloyd to write a letter. She groaned for days whenever she received one, because it had to be answered. But when Joyce went away she said, 'Now, Lloyd, I know I shall be homesick for Locust, and I want to hear every single thing that happens. Don't you dare send me a stingy two-page letter, half of it apologising for not writing sooner, and half of it promising to do better next time.

"'Just prop my picture up in front of you and look me in the eyes and begin to talk. Tell me all the little things that most people leave out ; what he said and she said on the way to the picnic, and how Betty looked in her daffodil dress, with the sun shining on her brown curls. Write as if you were making pictures for me, so that when I read I can see everything you are doing.'

"It was excellent advice, and as Joyce's letters were written in that way, Lloyd had a good model to copy. Joyce, being an artist, naturally makes pictures even of her letters. When Betty went away and began sending home such well-written accounts of her journey, I found that Lloyd's style improved constantly. She wrote a dear little letter to the Major, last week, telling all about Hero. I was surprised to see how prettily she expressed her appreciation of his gift."

Mr. Sherman took the letter and began to read. In two places he corrected a misspelled word, and here and there supplied missing commas and quotation marks. There was a gratified smile on his face when he finished. "That is certainly a lengthy letter for a twelve-year-old girl to write," he said, in a pleased tone, "and cannot fail to be interesting to Joyce. The letters she wrote me from the Cuckoo's Nest were stiff, short scrawls compared to this. I must tell my Little Colonel how proud I am of her improvement."

His words of praise were not spoken, however. He expressed his appreciation, later, by leaving on her table a box of foreign correspondence paper. It was of the best quality he could find in Tours, and to Lloyd's delight the monogram engraved on it was even prettier than Eugenia's.

"Why did Papa Jack write this on the first sheet in the box, mothah?" she asked, coming to her with a sentence written in her father's big, businesslike hand: '*There is no surer way to build a Road of the Loving Heart in the memory of absent friends, than to bridge the space between with the cheer and sympathy and good-will of friendly letters.*'

" Why did Papa Jack write that ? " she repeated.

" Because he saw your last letter to Joyce, and was so pleased with the improvement you have made," answered Mrs. Sherman. " He has given you a good text for your writing-desk."

" I'll paste it in the top," said Lloyd. "Then I can't lose it." " ' There is no surer way,' " she repeated to herself as she carried the box back to her room, " 'to bridge the space between . . . with the cheer and sympathy and good-will.' "

There flashed across her mind the thought of some one who needed cheer and sympathy far more than Joyce did, and who would welcome a friendly letter from her with its foreign stamp, as eagerly as if it were some real treasure. Jessie Nolan was the girl she thought of, an invalid with a crippled spine, to whom the dull days in her wheeled chair by the window seemed endless, and who had so little to brighten her monotonous life.

" I'll write her a note this minute," thought Lloyd, with a warm glow in her heart. " I'll describe some of the sights we have seen, and send her that fo' leafed clovah that I found at the château yestahday, undah a window of the great hall where Anne of Brittany was married ovah fo' hundred yeahs ago. I don't suppose Jessie gets a lettah once a yeah."

When that note was written, Lloyd thought of
Mom Beck and the pride that would shine in the
face of her old black nurse if she should receive a
letter from Europe, and how proudly it would be
carried around and displayed to all the coloured
people in the Valley. So with the kindly impulse
of her father's text still upon her, she dashed off a
note to her, telling her of some of her visits to the
palaces of bygone kings and queens.

Eugenia came in as she finished, but before she
closed her desk she jotted two names on a slip of
paper. Mrs. Waters's was one. She was a little old
Englishwoman, who did fine laundry work in the
Valley, and who was always talking about the
'awthorne 'edges in her old English home.

"I'll write to her from London," Lloyd thought.
"If we should get a sight of any of the royal family,
how tickled she would be to hear it."

The other name was Janet McDonald. She was
a sad, sweet-faced young teacher whom Miss Allison
always called her "Scotch lassie Jane." "I don't
suppose she'd care to get a letter from a little girl
like me," thought Lloyd, "but I know she'd love
to have a piece of heather from the hills near her
home. I'll send her a piece when we get up in
Scotland."

The letter that Eugenia sent to Joyce was only a short outline of her plans. She knew that the other girls had sent long accounts of their trip through Touraine, so hers was much shorter than usual.

"Papa has decided to send me to a school just outside of Paris this year," she wrote, "instead of the one in New York, so it will be a long time before I see my native land again. He will have to be over here several months, and can spend Christmas and Easter with me, so I can see him fully as often as I used to at home.

"It is a very select school. Madame recommends it highly, and I am simply delighted. A New York girl whom I know very well is to be there too, and we are looking forward to all sorts of larks. Thursday we are to start to London for a short tour of England and Scotland. Then the others are going home and papa and I shall go by Chester for my maid. Poor old Eliot has had a glorious vacation at home, she writes. She is to stay at the school with me. We shall be so busy until I get settled that I shall not have time to write soon; but no matter how far my letters may be apart, I am always your devoted   EUGENIA."

CHAPTER X.

ON THE WING

"Who is going away?" asked Lloyd, one afternoon, of the girls who were sitting in her room, manicuring their nails. "There goes a pile of trunks out to the baggage wagon."

As she spoke, a carriage drove up to the door of the hotel, and Fanchette went out with the poodle in her arms.

"The Sattawhites," answered Eugenia. "There's Howl and Henny climbing into the carriage, and, oh, look, girls! There comes Mrs. Sattawhite herself. I haven't had many glimpses of her. Isn't she gorgeous! You know they had to leave," she continued, turning to the girls. "I forgot to tell you what happened early this morning while you were down-town.

"I was up in my room writing to Joyce, when I heard a rumble and a running down in the back hall. Somebody called 'Fire! Fire!' Then somebody else took it up, and the old gentleman at the end of the hall, who never appears in public until noon, came bursting out of his room in his bath robe, his shoes in one hand and his false teeth in the other. It was the funniest sight! There was wild excitement for a few minutes. One woman began throwing things out of the window, and another stood and shrieked and wrung her hands.

" The waiter with the long black side-whiskers tore up-stairs and grabbed his arms full of those bottles in the racks — you know — those fire-extinguishing bottles that have some kind of chemical stuff in them. There was a strong smell of smoke and a little puff of it curling up from under the stairs. He threw all those bottles down into the lower hall. You can imagine the smash there was when they struck the stone floor.

" Papa rushed down to investigate, at the first alarm. He found that it was only Howl and Henny playing hook-and-ladder with a little red wagon. They had taken an old flannel blouse of Henny's and set fire to it. Howl explained that they did it because woollen rags make such a nice thick smoke, and last a long time, and when they yelled fire they were not to blame, he said, if other people didn't know that they were 'jes' a-playin', and went and yelled in earnest,'

"Papa took their part, and said that two boys with as much energy as they have must find an outlet somewhere, and that it was no wonder that they were restless, cooped up in a hotel day after day, with no amusement but their prim walks with the maid and the poodle. But the old gentleman who had been so frightened that he ran out in public without his teeth, and the woman who had thrown her toilet bottles out of the window and broken them, were furious. They complained to the landlord, and said that it was not the first offence. The boys were always annoying them.

"So the landlord had to go to Mrs. Sattawhite. She found out what the old gentleman said, that a mother who had to go travelling around all over Europe, giving her time and attention to society and a miserable poodle, had better put her children in an orphan asylum before she started. She was so indignant that I could hear her talking away down in the office. She said that she would leave the instant that Fanchette could get the trunks packed. So there they go."

Mrs. Sattawhite had sailed back to the office during the telling of Eugenia's story, so their departure was delayed a moment. When she came out again, Fidelia followed her sulkily. Just as they drove off, she looked up at the open window, and saw the girls, who were waving good-bye. Then a smile flickered across her sorry little face, for, moved by some sudden impulse, the Little Colonel leaned out and threw her a kiss.

"I suppose I'll nevah see her again," she said, thoughtfully, as the carriage rolled around a corner, out of sight. "I wish now that I had been niceah to her. We may both change evah so much by the time we are grown, yet if I live to be a hundred I'll always think of her as the girl who was so quarrelsome that the English lady groaned, 'Oh, those dreadful American children!' And I suppose she'll remembah me for the high and mighty way I tried to snub her whenevah I had a chance."

As she spoke there was a knock at the door, and a maid brought in a package for Lloyd. "Oh, look, girls!" she exclaimed, holding up a tiny pair of silver embroidery scissors, Fidelia's parting gift. They were evidently something that had been given her, for the little silver sheath into which they were thrust was beautifully engraved in old English letters with the name "*Fidelia*." Around them was wrapped a strip of rumpled paper on which was scrawled : "For you to remember me by. That day you took me to the Gate of the Giant Scissors was the best time I ever had."

"Poor little thing!" exclaimed Betty. "To think that she was afraid to go in, for fear that she didn't belong to the kingdom, and that the scissors might leap down and drive her back."

"Oh, if I had only known!" sighed Lloyd, remorsefully. "I feel too mean for anything! If I'd only believed that it was because she hadn't been brought up to know any bettah that she acted so horrid, and that all the time she really wanted to be liked! Mothah told me I ought to put myself in her place, and make allowances for her, but I didn't want to even try, and I nevah was nice to her but once — that time I gave her the candy. Then I was only pretendin' I cared for her, just for fun. I didn't want her to go with us to the Scissahs gate that day. Mothah made me invite her. I fussed about it. I'm goin' to write to her the minute I finish polishin' my nails, and tell her how sorry I am that I didn't leave a kindah memory behind me."

They rubbed away in silence for a few minutes, then Lloyd spoke again. "I suahly have enough things now to remind me about the memory roads I am tryin' to leave behind me for everybody. Every time I look at this little ring it says 'A Road of the

Loving Heart.' And the scissahs will recall the fairy tale. It was only unselfish service that kept them bright and shining, and only those who belonged to the kingdom of loving hearts could go in at the gate. Then there's the Red Cross of Geneva on Hero's collah — there couldn't be a moah beautiful memory than the one left by all who have wo'n that Red Cross."

"Yes," said Betty, holding up a hand to inspect the pink finger nails now polished to her satisfaction. "And there is the white flower that the two little Knights of Kentucky wear. Keith said that his badge meant the same thing to him that my ring does to me. Their motto is 'Right the wrong.' That's what the Giant Scissors always did, and that's what Robert Louis Stevenson tried to do for the Samoan chiefs. That is why they loved him and built the road."

"Funny, how they all sing the same song," said Eugenia. "It's just the same, only they sing it in different keys."

After Betty and Eugenia had gone to their rooms, Lloyd sat a long time toying with the silver scissors, before writing her note of acknowledgment. The sheath was of hammered silver, and around the name was a beautifully wrought design of tiny clustered grapes.

"It is one of the prettiest things that my wondah-ball has unrolled," she said to herself, "and it has certainly taught me a lesson. Poah little Fidelia! If I'd only known that she cared, there were lots of times that she could have gone with us, and it would have made her so happy. If I had only put myself in her place when mothah told me! But I was so cross and hateful I enjoyed bein' selfish. Now all the bein' sorry in the world won't change things!"

It would be too much like a guide-book if this story were to give a record of the next two weeks. Betty's good-times book was filled, down to the last line on the last page, and the partnership diary had to have several extra leaves pasted inside the cover. From morning until night there was a constant round of sightseeing. The shops and streets of London first, the Abbey and the Tower, a hundred places that they had read about and longed to see, and after they had seen, longed to come back to for another visit.

"We can only take a bird's-eye view now and hurry on, but we must certainly come back some other summer," said Mr. Sherman, when Lloyd wanted to linger in the Tower of London among the armour and weapons that had been worn by the old knights, centuries ago. He repeated it when Betty

looked back longingly at the Poets' Corner in West-
minster Abbey, where the great organ was echoing
down the solemn aisles, and again when Eugenia
begged for another coach ride out to Hampton
Court.

> "'Gay go up and gay go down
>   To ring the bells of London town,"

sang the Little Colonel. "I am having such a good
time that I'd like to stay on right heah all the rest
of the summah."

But she thought that about nearly every other
place they visited, Windsor, and Warwick Castle, and
Shakespeare's birthplace, — the quaint little village
on the Avon ; Ambleside, where they took the coach
for long rides among the lakes made famous by the
poets who lived among them and made them immor-
tal with their songs.

From these English lakes to Scottish moors, from
the land of hawthorne to the land of heather, from
low green meadows where the larks sang, to the high-
lands where plaided shepherds watched their flocks,
they went with enthusiasm that never waned. They
found the "banks and braes o' Bonnie Doon," and
wandered along the banks of more than one little
river that they had loved for years in song and story.

"Haven't we learned a lot !" exclaimed Eugenia,

as they journeyed back by rail to Liverpool, where
the Shermans and Betty were to take the steamer.
"I'm sure that I've learned ten times as much as I
would in school, this last year."

"And had such a lovely time in the bargain,"
added Lloyd. "It's goin' to make a difference in
the way I study this wintah, and in what I read. If
we evah come ovah heah again, I intend to know
something about English history. Then the places
we visit will be so much moah interestin'. I'll not
spend so much time on fairy tales and magazine stories. I'm goin' to make my reading count for something aftah this. It was dreadfully mawtifyin' to
find out that I was so ignorant, and how much there
is in the world to know, that I had nevah even heard
of."

That afternoon, in the big Liverpool hotel, the
trunks were packed for the last time.

"Seems something like the night befo' Christmas,"
said the Little Colonel, as she counted the packages
piled on the floor beside her trunk. They were the
presents that she had chosen for the friends at home.

"Nineteen, twenty," she went on counting, "and
that music box for Mom Beck makes twenty-one,
and the souvenir spoons for the Walton girls make
twenty-five. Oh, I didn't show you these," she said.

"This is Allison's," she explained, opening a little box. "See the caldron and the bells on the handle? I got this in Denmark. That's from Andersen's tale of the swineherd's magic kettle, you know. Kitty's is from Tam O'Shanter's town. That's why there is a witch and a broomstick engraved on it. This spoon for Elise came from Berne. I think that's a darling little bear's head on the handle. What did you get, Betty?" she continued, turning to her suddenly. "You haven't shown me a single thing."

Betty laid down the spoons she was admiring. "You'll not think they are worth carrying home," she said, slowly. "I couldn't buy handsome presents like yours, you know, so I just picked up little things here and there, that wouldn't be worth anything at all if they hadn't come from famous places."

"Show them to me, anyhow," persisted Lloyd.

Betty untied a small box. "It's only a handful of lava," she explained, "that I picked up on Vesuvius. But Davy will like it because he thinks a volcano is such a wonderful thing. Here are some pebbles the boys will be interested in, because I found them on the field of Waterloo. They are making collections of such things, and Waterloo is a long way from the Cuckoo's Nest. They haven't any foreign things at all.

" I wanted to take something nice to Miss Allison, but I couldn't afford to buy anything fine enough. So I just pressed these buttercups that grew by the gate of Anne Hathaway's cottage. See how sun-shiny and satiny they are ? Cousin Carl gave me a photograph of the cottage, and I fastened the butter-cups here on the side. I couldn't offer such a little gift to some people, but Miss Allison is the kind that appreciates the thought that prompts a gift more than the thing itself."

There were a few more photographs, a handker-chief for Mom Beck, and a string of cheap Venetian beads for May Lily. The most expensive article in the collection was a little mosaic pin for her Cousin Hetty. "I got that in Venice," said Betty. "Cousin Hetty hasn't a single piece of jewelry to her name, and she never gets any presents but plain, useful things, so I am sure she will be pleased."

Lloyd turned away, thinking of the great contrast between her gifts and Betty's, and wishing that she had not made such a display of hers.

"If I were in Betty's place," she said to herself, "I'd be so jealous of me that I could hardly stand it. She's just a little orphan alone in the world, and I have mothah and Papa Jack and Hero and Tarbaby for my very own."

But the Little Colonel need not have wasted any sympathy on Betty. While one stowed away her expensive presents in her trunk, the other wrapped up her little souvenirs, humming softly to herself. It would have been hard to find anywhere in the queen's dominion, a happier child than Betty, as she sat beside her trunk, thinking of the beautiful journey with Cousin Carl, just ending, and the life awaiting her at Locust with her godmother and the Little Colonel. There was only one cloud on her horizon, and that was the parting with Eugenia and her father.

That last evening they spent together in the private parlour adjoining Mrs. Sherman's room. Early after dinner Lloyd and her father went down to pay a visit to Hero, and see that he was properly cared for. He had had a hard time since reaching England, for the laws regarding the quarantining of dogs are strict, and it had taken many shillings on Mr. Sherman's part and some tears on the Little Colonel's to procure him the privileges he had.

"The whole party will be glad when he is safely landed in Kentucky, I am sure," said Mrs. Sherman, as the door closed after them. "I'd never consent to take another dog on such a journey, after all the trouble and expense this one has been. Lloyd is so devoted to him that she is heartbroken if he has to be tied up or made uncomfortable in any way. She'll probably come up-stairs in tears to-night because he wants to follow her, and must be kept a prisoner."

While they waited for her return, Mrs. Sherman drew Eugenia into her room for a last confidential talk, and Betty, nestling beside Cousin Carl on the sofa, tried to thank him for all his fatherly kindness to her on their long pilgrimage together. But he would not let her put her gratitude in words. His answer was the same that it had been that last night of the house party, when, looking down the locust avenue gleaming with its myriad of lights, like some road to the City of the Shining Ones, she had cried out : "Oh, *why* is everybody so good to me ? "

The others came in presently, and the evening seemed to be on wings, it flew so swiftly, as they planned for another summer to be spent at Locust, when Eugenia should come home from her year in the Paris school. And never, it seemed, were good nights followed so quickly by good mornings, or good mornings by good-byes.

Almost before they realised that the parting time had actually come, the Little Colonel and Betty were leaning over the railing of the great steamer, waving their handkerchiefs to Eugenia and her father on the dock. Smaller and smaller grew the familiar outlines, wider and wider the distance between the ship and the shore, until at last even Eugenia's red jacket faded into a mere speck, and it was no longer of any use to wave good-bye.

CHAPTER XI.

HOMEWARD BOUND

On that long, homeward journey it was well for Hero that he wore the Red Cross on his collar. The little symbol was the open sesame to many a privilege that ordinary dogs are not allowed on shipboard. Instead of being confined to the hold, he was given the liberty of the ship, and when his story was known he received as much flattering attention as if he had been some titled nobleman.

The captain shook the big white paw, gravely put into nis hand at the Little Colonel's bidding, and then stooped to stroke the dog's head. As he looked into the wistful, intelligent eyes his own grew tender.

"I have a son in the service," he said, "sent back from South Africa, covered with scars. I know what that Red Cross meant to him for a good many long weeks. Go where you like, old fellow! The ship is yours, so long as you make no trouble."

"Oh, thank you!" cried the Little Colonel, looking up at the big British captain with a beaming face. "I'd rathah be tied up myself than to have Hero kept down there in the hold. I'm suah he'll not bothah anybody."

Nor did he. No one from stoker to deck steward could make the slightest complaint against him, so dignified and well behaved was he. Lloyd was proud of him and his devotion. Wherever she went he followed her, lying at her feet when she sat in her steamer-chair, walking close beside her when she and Betty promenaded the deck.

Everybody stopped to speak to him, and to question Lloyd and Betty about him, so that it was not many days before the little girls and the great St. Bernard had made friends of all the passengers who were able to be on deck.

The hours are long at sea, and people gladly welcome anything that provides entertainment, so Lloyd and Betty were often called aside as they walked, and invited to join some group, and tell to a knot of interested listeners all they knew of Hero and the Major, and the training of the French ambulance dogs.

In return Lloyd's stories nearly always called forth some anecdote from her listeners about the Red Cross work in America, and to her great surprise she found five persons among them who had met Clara

Barton in some great national calamity of fire, flood, or pestilence.

One was a portly man with a gruff voice, who had passed through the experiences of the forest fires that swept through Michigan, over twenty years ago. As he told his story, he made the scenes so real that the children forgot where they were. They could almost smell the thick, stifling smoke of the burning forest, hear the terrible crackling of the flames, feel the scorching heat in their faces, and see the frightened cattle driven into the lakes and streams by the pursuing fire.

They listened with startled eyes as he described the wall of flame, hemming in the peaceful home where his little son played around the door-step. They held their breath while he told of their mad flight from it, when, lashing his horses into a gallop, he looked back to see it licking up everything in the world he held dear except the frightened little family huddled at his feet. He had worked hard to build the cottage. It was furnished with family heirlooms brought West with them from the old homestead in Vermont. It was hard to see those great red tongues devouring it in a mouthful.

In the morning, although they had reached a place of safety, they were out in a charred, blackened wilderness, without a roof to shelter them, a chair to sit on, or a crust to eat. "The hardest thing to bear," he said, "was to hear my little three-year-old Bertie begging for his breakfast, and to know that there was nothing within miles of us to satisfy his hunger, and that the next day it would be the same, and the next, and the next.

"We were powerless to help ourselves. But while we sat there in utter despair, a neighbour rode by and hailed us. He told us that Red Cross committees had started out from Milwaukee and Chicago at first tidings of the fire, with car-loads of supplies, and that if we could go to the place where they were distributing we could get whatever we needed.

"I wish you could have seen what they were handing out when we got there: tools and lumber to put up cabins, food and beds and clothes and coal-oil. They'd thought of everything and provided everything, and they went about the distributing in a systematic, businesslike way that somehow put heart and cheer into us all.

"They didn't make us feel as if they were handing out alms to paupers, but as if they were helping some of their own family on to their feet again, and putting them in shape to help themselves. Even my little Bertie felt it. Young as he was, he never for-

got that awful night when we fled from the fire, nor
the hungry day that followed, nor the fact that the
arm that carried him food, when he got it at last,
wore a brassard marked like that." He touched the
Red Cross on Hero's collar.

"And when the chance came to show the same
brotherly spirit to some one else in trouble and pass
the help along, he was as ready as the rest of us to
do his share.

"Three years afterward I read in the papers of
the floods that had swept through the Ohio and Mississippi valleys, and of the thousands that were home-
less. Bertie, — he was six then, — he listened to the
account of the children walking the streets, crying
because they hadn't a roof over them or anything to
eat. He didn't say a word, but he climbed up to the
mantel and took down his little red savings-bank.

"We were pretty near on our feet again by that
time, although we were still living in a cabin. The
crops had been good, and we had been able to save a
little. He poured out all the pennies and nickels in
his bank, — ninety-three cents they came to, — and
then he got his only store toy, a box of tin soldiers
that had been sent to him Christmas, and put that
on the table beside the money. We didn't appear to
notice what he was doing. Presently he brought the

mittens his grandmother up in Vermont had knit for him. Then he waited a bit, and seemed to be weighing something in his mind. By and by he slipped away to the chest where his Sunday clothes were kept and took them out, new suit, shoes, cap and all, and laid them on the table with the money and the tin soldiers.

" ' There, daddy,' he said, ' tell the Red Cross people to send them to some little boy like me, that's been washed out of his home and hasn't anything of toys left, or his clothes.'

" I tell you it made a lump come up in my throat to see that the little fellow had taken his very best to pay his debt of gratitude. Nothing was too great for him to sacrifice. Even his tin soldiers went when he remembered what the Red Cross had done for him."

" My experience with the Red Cross was in the Mississippi floods of '82," said a gentleman who had joined the party. " One winter day we were attracted by screams out in the river, and found that they came from some people who were floating down on a house that had been washed away. There they were, that freezing weather, out in the middle of the river, their clothes frozen on them, ill from fright and exposure. I went out in one of the boats that was sent to their rescue, and helped bring them to shore. I was so impressed by the tales of suffering they told that I went up the river to investigate.

"At every town, and nearly every steamboat landing, I found men from the relief committees already at work, distributing supplies. They didn't stop when they had provided food and clothing. They furnished seed by the car-load to the farmers, just as in the Galveston disaster, a few years ago, they furnished thousands of strawberry plants to the people who were wholly dependent on their crops for their next year's food."

"Where did they get all those stores?" asked Lloyd. "And the seeds and the strawberry plants?"

"Most of it was donated," answered the gentleman. "Many contributions come pouring in after such a disaster, just as little Bertie's did. But the society is busy all the time, collecting and storing away the things that may be needed at a moment's notice. People would contribute, of course, even if there were no society to take charge of their donations, but without its wise hands to distribute, much would be lost.

"A number of years ago a physician in Bedford, Indiana, gave a tract of land to the American National Red Cross; more than a square mile, I believe, a beautiful farm with buildings and fruit-trees, a place where material can be accumulated and stored. By the terms of the treaty of Geneva, forty nations are pledged to hold it sacred for ever against all invading armies, to the use of the Red Cross. It is the only spot on earth pledged to perpetual peace."

It was from a sad-faced lady in black, who had had two sons drowned in the Johnstown flood, that Lloyd and Betty heard the description of Clara Barton's five months' labour there. A doctor's wife who had been in the Mt. Vernon cyclone, and a newspaper man who had visited the South Carolina islands after the tidal wave, and Charleston after the earthquake, piled up their accounts of those scenes of suffering, some of them even greater than the horrors of war, so that Lloyd could not sleep that night, for thinking of them.

"Betty," she whispered, across the stateroom, turning over in her berth. "Betty, are you awake?"

"Yes. Do you want anything?"

"I can't sleep. That's all. Every time I shut my eyes I see all those awful things they told about: cities in ruins, and dead people lying around in piles, and the yellow fevah camps, and floods and fiah. It is a dreadful world, Betty. No one knows what awful thing is goin' to happen next."

"Don't think about the dreadful part," urged Betty. "Think of the funny things Mrs. Brown told, of the time the levee broke at Shawneetown. The table all set for supper, and the water pouring in until the table floated up to the ceiling, and went bobbing around like a fish."

"That doesn't help any," said Lloyd, after a moment. "I see the watah crawlin' highah and highah up the walls, above the piano and pictuahs, till I feel as if it is crawlin' aftah me, and will be all ovah the bed in a minute. Did you evah think how solemn it is, Betty Lewis, to be away out in the middle of the ocean, with nothing but a few planks between us and drownin'? Seems to me the ship pitches around moah than usual, to-night, and the engine makes a mighty strange, creakin' noise."

"Do you remember the night I put you to sleep at the Cuckoo's Nest?" asked Betty. "The night after you fell down the barn stairs, playing barley-bright? Shut your eyes and let me try it again."

It was no nursery legend or border ballad that Betty crooned this time, but some peaceful lines of the old Quaker poet, and the quiet comfort of them stole into Lloyd's throbbing brain and soothed her excited fancy. Long after Betty was asleep she went on repeating to herself the last lines:

" I know not where His islands lift
Their fronded palms in air,
I only know I cannot drift
Beyond His love and care."

She did dream of fires and floods that night, but the horror of the scenes was less, because a baby voice called cheerfully through them, " Here, daddy, give these to the poor little boys that are cold and homesick; " and a great St. Bernard, with a Red Cross on his back, ran around distributing mittens and tin soldiers.

" Now that we are half-way across the ocean," said Mrs. Sherman, next morning, " I may give you Allison Walton's letter.   She enclosed it in one her mother wrote, and asked me not to give it to you until we were in mid-ocean.   I suppose her experience in coming over from Manila taught her that letters are more appreciated then than at the beginning of the voyage."

The Little Colonel unfolded it, exclaiming in surprise, " It is dated ' *The Beeches*.' I thought that they were in Lloydsboro Valley all summah, in the cottage next to the churchyard.   That one you used to like," she added, turning to Betty.   " The one with the high green roof and deah little diamond-shaped window-panes."

"So they are in the Valley," answered her mother. "But their new house is finished now, and they have moved into that. As they have left all the beautiful beech grove standing around it, they have decided to call the place The Beeches, as ours is called Locust, on account of the trees in front of it."

Beckoning to Betty to come and listen, Lloyd sat down to read the letter, and Mrs. Sherman turned to an acquaintance next her. "It is General Walton's family of whom we were speaking," she explained. "Since his death in Manila they have been living in Louisville, until recently. We are so delighted to think that they have now come to the Valley to live. It was Mrs. Walton's home in her girlhood, and her mother's place, Edgewood, is just across the avenue from The Beeches. Lloyd and the little girls are the best of friends, and we are all interested in Ranald, the only son. He was the youngest captain in the army, you know. He received his appointment and was under fire before he was twelve years old."

"Oh, mothah," spoke up Lloyd, so eagerly that she did not notice that she had interrupted the conversation. "Listen to this, please. You know I wrote to Allison about Hero, and this lettah is neahly all about him. She said her fathah knew Clara Barton, and that in Cuba and Manila the games and books that the Red Cross sent to the hospitals were appreciated by the soldiahs almost as much as the delicacies. And she says her mothah thinks it would be fine for us all to start a fund for the Red Cross. They wanted to get up a play because they're always havin' tableaux and such things.

"They've been readin' ' Little Women ' again, and Jo's Christmas play made them want to do something like that. They can have all the shields and knights' costumes that the MacIntyre boys had when they gave Jonesy's benefit. They were going to have an entahtainment last week, but couldn't agree. Allison wanted to play ' Cinda'ella,' because there are such pretty costumes in that, but Kitty wanted to make up one all about witches and spooks and robbah-dens, and call it ' The One-Eyed Ghost of Cocklin Tower.'

"She wanted to be the ghost. They've decided to wait till we get home befo' they do anything."

"There's your opportunity, Betty," said Mrs. Sherman, turning to her goddaughter with a smile. "Why can't you distinguish yourself by writing a play that will make us all proud of you, and at the same time swell the funds of the Red Cross?"

"Oh, do you really think I could, godmother?

Are you in earnest?" cried Betty, her face shining with pleasure.

"Entirely so," answered Mrs. Sherman, running her hand caressingly over Betty's brown hair. "This little curly head is full of all sorts of tales of goblins and ogres and witches and fairy folk. String them together, dear, in some sort of shape, and I'll help with the costumes."

The suggestion was made playfully, but Betty looked dreamily out to sea, her face radiant. The longing to do something to please her godmother and make her proud of her was the first impulse that thrilled her, but as she began to search her brain for a plot, the joy of the work itself made her forget everything else, even the passing of time. She was amazed when Lloyd called to her that they were going down to lunch. She had sat the entire morning wrapped in her steamer-rug, looking out across the water with far-seeing eyes. As the blue waves rose and fell, her thoughts had risen and swayed to their rhythmic motion, and begun to shape themselves into rhyme. Line after line was taking form, and she wished impatiently that Lloyd had not called her. How could one be hungry when some inward power, past understanding, was making music in one's soul?

She followed Lloyd down to the table like one in a trance, but the spell was broken for awhile by Lloyd's persistent chatter.

"You know there's all sort of things you could have," she suggested, "if you wanted to use them in the piece. Tarbaby and the Filipino pony, and we could even borrow the beah from Fairchance if you wanted anything like Beauty and the Beast. We had that once though, at Jonesy's benefit, so maybe you wouldn't want to use it again."

"There's to be a knight in it," answered Betty, "and he'll be mounted in one scene. So we may need one of the ponies." Then she turned to her godmother. "Do you suppose there is a spinning-wheel anywhere in the neighbourhood that we could borrow?"

"Yes, I have one of my great-grandmother's stored away in the trunk-room. You may have that."

The Little Colonel shrugged her shoulders impatiently. "Oh, I can't wait to know what you're goin' to do with a spinnin'-wheel in the play. Tell me now, Betty."

But the little playwright only shook her head. "I'm not sure myself yet. But I keep thinking of the humming of the wheel, and a sort of spinning-song keeps running through my head. I thought, too, it would help to make a pretty scene."

"You're goin' to put Hero in it, aren't you?" was the Little Colonel's question.

"Oh, Lloyd! I can't," cried Betty, in dismay. "A dog couldn't have a part with princes and witches and fairies."

"I don't see why not," persisted Lloyd. "I sha'n't take half the interest if he isn't in it. I think you might put him in, Betty," she urged. "I'd do as much for you, if it was something you had set your heart on. *Please*, Betty!" she begged.

"But he won't fit anywhere!" said Betty, in a distressed tone. "I'd put him in, gladly, if he'd only go, but, don't you see, Lloyd, he isn't appropriate. It would spoil the whole thing to drag him in."

"I don't see why," said Lloyd, a trifle sharply. "Isn't it going to be a Red Cross entahtainment, and isn't Hero a Red Cross dog? I think it's *very* appropriate for him to have a part, even one of the principal ones."

"I can't think of a single thing for him to do —" began Betty.

"You can if you try hard enough," insisted Lloyd.

Betty sighed hopelessly, and turned to her lunch in silence. She wanted to please the Little Colonel, but it seemed impossible to her to give Hero a part without spoiling the entertainment.

"Maybe some of the books in the ship's library might help you," said Mr. Sherman, who had been an amused listener. "I'll look over some of them for you."

Later in the day he came up to Betty where she stood leaning against the deck railing. He laid a book upon it, open at a picture of seven white swans. "Do you remember this?" he asked. "The seven brothers who were changed to swans, and the good sister who wove a coat for each one out of flax she spun from the churchyard nettles? The magic coats gave them back their human forms. Maybe you can use the same idea, and have your prince changed into a dog for awhile."

"Oh, thank you!" she cried. "I'd forgotten that story. I am sure it will help."

He walked away, leaving her poring over the picture, but presently, as he paced the deck, he felt her light touch on his arm, and turned to see her glowing little face looking up into his.

"I've got it!" she cried. "The picture made me think of the very thing. I had been fumbling with a tangled skein, trying to find a place to begin unwinding. Now you have given me the starting thread, and it all begins to smooth out beautifully. I'm going for pencil and paper now, to write it all down before I forget."

That pencil and note-book were her constant companions the rest of the voyage. Sometimes Lloyd, coming upon her suddenly, would hear her whispering a list of rhymes such as more, core, pour, store, shore, before, or creature, teacher, feature, at which they would both laugh and Betty exclaim, hopelessly, "I can't find a word to fit that place." At other times Lloyd passed her in respectful silence, for she knew by the rapt look on Betty's face that the mysterious business of verse-making was proceeding satisfactorily, and she dared not interrupt.

The day they sighted land, Lloyd exclaimed: "Oh, I can hardly wait to get home! I've had a perfectly lovely summah, and I've enjoyed every mile of the journey, but the closah I get to Locust the moah it seems to me that the very nicest thing my wondah-ball can unroll (except givin' me Hero, of co'se) is the goin' back home."

"Your wonder-ball," repeated Betty, who knew the birthday story. "That gives me an idea. The princess shall have a wonder-ball in the play."

Lloyd laughed. "I believe that's all you think about nowadays, Betty. Put up yoah scribblin' for awhile and come and watch them swing the trunks up out of the hold. We're almost home, Betty Lewis, almost home!"

CHAPTER XII.

HOME AGAIN

MEANWHILE in Lloydsboro Valley the summer had slipped slowly by. Locust seemed strangely quiet with the great front gates locked, and never any sound of wheels or voices coming down the avenue. Judge Moore's place was closed also, and Tanglewood, just across the way, had been opened only a few weeks in the spring. So birds and squirrels held undisputed possession of that part of the Valley, and the grass grew long and the vines climbed high, and often the soft whisper of the leaves was the only sound to be heard.

But in the shady beech grove, next the churchyard, and across the avenue from Mrs. MacIntyre's, the noise of hammer and saw and trowel had gone on unceasingly, until at last the new home was ready for its occupants. The family did not have far to move to "The Beeches"; only over the stile from the quaint green-roofed cottage next door, where they had spent the summer.

Allison, Kitty, and Elise climbed back and forth over the stile, their arms full of their particular treasures, which they could not trust to the moving-vans. All the week that Betty and Lloyd were tossing out on the ocean, they were flitting about the new house, growing accustomed to its unfamiliar corners. By the time the *Majestic* steamed into the New York harbour, they were as much at home in their new surroundings as if they had always lived there. The tent was pitched on the lawn, the large family of dolls was brought out under the trees, and the games, good times, and camp-fire cooking went on as if they had never been interrupted for an instant by the topsy-turvy work of moving.

"Whose day is it for the pony-cart?" asked Mrs. Walton, coming out on the steps one morning.

"It was mine," answered Kitty, speaking up from the hammock, where she swung, half in, half out, watching a colony of ants crawling along the ground underneath. "But I traded my turn to Elise, for her biggest paper boy doll."

"And I traded my turn to Allison, if she would let me use all the purple and yellow paint I want in her paint-box, while I am making my Princess Pansy's ball dress," said Elise.

Mrs. Walton smiled at the transfer of rights. The

little girls had an arrangement by which they took
turns in using the cart certain days in the week,
when Ranald did not want to ride his Filipino pony.

"Whoever has it to-day may do an errand for me,"
Mrs. Walton said, adding, as she turned toward the
house, "Do you know that Lloyd and Betty are
coming on the three o'clock train this afternoon?"

"Then I don't want the pony-cart," exclaimed
Allison, quickly. "I'm going down to the depot to
meet them."

The depot was in sight of The Beeches, not more
than three minutes' walk distant.

"Can't go back on your trade!" sang out Elise.
"Can't go back on your trade!"

"Oh, you take it, Elise," coaxed Allison. "It's
my regular turn to-morrow. I'll make some fudge
in the morning, if you will."

Elise considered a moment. "Well," she said,
finally, "I'll let you off from your trade if Kitty will
let me off from mine."

"No, *sir!*" answered Kitty. "A trade's a trade.
I want that paper boy doll."

"But it's your regular turn," coaxed Elise, "and
I'd much rather go down to the depot to meet the
girls than go riding."

"So would I," said Kitty, spurring the procession

of ants to faster speed with her slipper toe.   Then ,
she sat up and considered the matter a moment.

"Oh, well," she said, presently, "I don't care,
after all.   If it will oblige you any I'll let you off,
and take the pony myself."

"Oh, thank you, sister," cried Elise.

"They'll only be at the depot a few minutes," continued the wily Kitty.   "So I'll drive down to meet
them in style in the cart, and then I'll go up to
Locust with them, beside the carriage, and hear all
about the trip first of anybody."

"I wish I'd thought of that," said Elise, a shade
of disappointment in her big dark eyes.

"I'll tell you," proposed Allison, enthusiastically.
"We'll *all* go down in the pony-cart to meet them
together.   That would be the nicest way to do."

"Oh!" was Kitty's cool reply, "I had thought
of going by for Katy or Corinne."   Then, seeing the
disappointment in the faces opposite, she added,
"But maybe I might change my mind.   Have you
got anything to trade for a chance to go?"

This transfer of possessions which they carried
on was like a continuous game, of which they never
tired, because of its endless variety.   It was a source
of great amusement to the older members of the
family.

"It is a mystery to me," said Miss Allison, "how they manage to keep track of their property, and remember who is the owner. I have known a doll or a dish to change hands half a dozen times in the course of a forenoon."

Elise promptly offered the paper boy doll again, which was promptly accepted. Allison had nothing to offer which Kitty considered equivalent to a seat in the cart, but by a roundabout transfer the trade was finally made. Allison gave Elise the amount of purple and yellow paint she needed for the Princess Pansy's ball gown, in return for which Elise gave her a piece of spangled gauze which Kitty had long had an eye upon. Allison in turn handed the gauze to Kitty for her right to a seat in the pony-cart, and the affair was thus happily settled to the satisfaction of all parties.

"It *isn't* that we are selfish with each other," Allison had retorted, indignantly, one day when Corinne remarked that she didn't see how sisters who loved each other could be so particular about everything. "It's only with our toys and the cart that we do that way. It's a kind of game that we've played always, and *we* think it's lots of fun."

So it happened that that afternoon, when the train stopped at Lloydsboro Valley, the first thing the

Little Colonel saw was the pony-cart drawn close to the platform. Then three little girls in white dresses and fresh ribbons, smiling broadly under their big flower-wreathed hats, sprang out to give them a warm welcome home, with enthusiastic hugs and kisses.

Hero's turn came next. Released from his long, tiresome confinement in the baggage-car, he came bounding into their midst, almost upsetting the Little Colonel in his joy at having his freedom again. He put out his great paw to each of the little girls in turn as Lloyd bade him shake hands with his new neighbours, but he growled suspiciously when Walker came up and laid black fingers upon him. He had never seen a coloured man before.

It was Betty's first meeting with the Walton girls. She had looked forward to it eagerly, first because they were the daughters of a man whom her little hero-loving heart honoured as one of the greatest generals of the army, who had given his life to his country, and died bravely in its service, and secondly because Lloyd's letters the winter before had been full of their sayings and doings. Mrs. Sherman, too, had told her many things of their life in Manila, and she felt that children who had such unusual experiences could not fail to be interesting. There was a third reason, however, that she scanned each face so closely. She had given them parts in the new play, and she was wondering how well they would fit those parts.

They in turn cast many inquiring glances at Betty, for they had heard all about this little song-bird that had been taken away from the Cuckoo's Nest. They had read her poem on " Night," which was published in a real paper, and they could not help looking upon her with a deep feeling of respect, tinged a little with awe, that a twelve-year-old girl could write verses good enough to be published. They had heard Keith's enthusiastic praises of her.

"Betty's a brick!" he had said, telling of several incidents of the house party, especially the picnic at the old mill, when she had gone so far to keep her "sacred promise." "She's the very nicest girl I know," he had added, emphatically, and that was high praise, coming from the particular Keith, who judged all girls by the standard of his mother.

As soon as the trunks were attended to, Mr. Sherman led the way to the carriage, waiting on the other side of the platform. Hero was given a place beside Walker, and although he sprang up obediently when he was bidden, he eyed his companion suspiciously all the way. The pony-cart trundled along beside the carriage, the girls calling back and forth to each other, above the rattle of the wheels.

"Oh, isn't Hero the loveliest dog that ever was! But you ought to see our puppy — the cutest thing — nothing but a bunch of soft, woozy curls." . . . "We're in the new house now, you must come over to-morrow." . . . "Mother is going to take us all camping soon. You are invited, too." This from the pony-cart in high-pitched voices in different keys.

"Oh, I've had a perfectly lovely time, and I've brought you all something in my trunk. And say, girls, Betty is writing a play for the Red Cross entertainment. There's a witch in it, Kitty, and lots of pretty costumes, Allison. And, oh, deah, I'm so glad to get home I don't know what to do first!" This from the carriage.

The great entrance gates were unlocked now, the lawn smoothly cut, the green lace-work of vines trimly trained around the high white pillars of the porches. The pony-cart turned back at the gate, and the carriage drove slowly up the avenue alone. The mellow sunlight of the warm September afternoon filtered down like gold, through the trees arching overhead.

"'Oh, the sun shines bright on my old Kentucky home,'" sang Lloyd, softly, leaning out of the car-

"BETTY SLOWLY FOLLOWED HER GODMOTHER UP THE
WIDE STAIRS"

riage to wave her hand to Mom Beck, who, in whitest of aprons and gayest of head bandanas, stood smiling and curtseying on the steps. The good old black face beamed with happiness as she cried, " Heah comes my baby, an' li'l' Miss Betty, too, bless her soul an' body ! "

Around the house came May Lily and a tribe of little pickaninnies, who fell back at sight of Hero leaping out of the carriage. He was the largest dog they had ever seen. Lloyd called them all around her and made them each shake hands with the astonished St. Bernard, who did not seem to relish this part of his introduction to Kentucky.

" He'll soon get used to you," said the Little Colonel. " May Lily, you run tell Aunt Cindy to give you a cooky or a piece of chicken for him to eat. Henry Clay, you bring a pan of watah. If you all fly around and wait on him right good, he'll like you lots bettah."

Leaving Lloyd to offer Hero the hospitality of Locust in the midst of her little black admirers, Betty slowly followed her godmother up the wide stairs.

" You're to have the same white and gold room again, dear," said Mrs. Sherman, peeping in as she passed the door. " I see that it is all in readiness. So walk in and take possession."

Betty was glad that she was alone, those first few minutes, the joy of the home-coming was so keen. Going in, she shut the door and gave a swift glance all around, from the dark polished floor, with its white angora rugs, to the filmy white curtains at the open casement windows. Everything was just as she had seen it last, — the dear little white dressing-table, with its crystal candlesticks, that always made her think of twisted icicles; the little heart-shaped pincushion and all the dainty toilet articles of ivory and gold; the pictures on the wall; the freshly gathered plumes of goldenrod in the crystal bowl on the mantel. She stood a moment, looking out of the open window, and thinking of the year that had gone by since she last stood in that room. Many a long and perilous mile she had travelled, but here she was back in safety, and instead of bandaged eyes and the horror of blindness hovering over her, she was able to look out on the beautiful world with strong, far-seeing sight.

The drudgery of the Cuckoo's Nest was far behind her now, and the bare little room under the eaves. Henceforth this was to be her home. She remembered the day in the church when her god-mother's invitation to the house party reached her, and just as she had knelt then in front of the narrow, bench-like altar, she knelt now, beside the little white bed. Now, as then, the late afternoon sun streamed across her brown curls and shining face, and " *Thank you, dear God*," came in the same grateful whisper from the depths of the same glad little heart.

"Betty! Betty!" called Lloyd, under her window. "Come and take a run over the place. I want to show Hero his new home."

Tired of sitting still so long on the cars, Betty was glad to join in the race over the smooth lawn and green meadows. Out in the pasture, Tarbaby waited by the bars. The grapevine swing in the mulberry-tree, every nook and corner where the guests of the house party had romped and played the summer before, seemed to hold a special greeting for them, and every foot of ground in old Locust seemed dearer for their long absence.

The next morning, when Tarbaby was led around for Lloyd to take her usual ride, both girls gave a cry of delight, for another pony followed close at his heels. It was the one that had been kept for Betty's use during the house party.

"It is Lad!" called the Little Colonel, excitedly. "Oh, Papa Jack! Is he goin' to stay heah all the time?"

"Yes, he belongs here now," answered Mr. Sher-man. "I want both my little girls to be well mounted, and to ride every day."

He motioned to a card hanging from Lad's bridle, and, leaning over, Lloyd read aloud, "For Betty from Papa Jack."

Betty could hardly realise her good fortune.

"Is he really mine?" she insisted, "the same as Tarbaby is Lloyd's?"

"Really yours, and just the same," answered Mr. Sherman, holding out his hand to help her mount.

She tried to thank him, tried to tell him how happy the gift had made her, but words could not measure either her gratitude or her pleasure. He read them both, however, in her happy face. As he swung her into the saddle, she leaned forward, saying, "I want to whisper something in your ear, Mr. Sher-man." As he bent his head she whispered, "Thank you for writing Papa Jack on the card. That made me happier than anything else."

"That is what I want you to call me always now, my little daughter," he answered, kissing her lightly on the cheek. "Locust is your home now, and you belong to all of us. Your godmother, the Little Colonel, and I each claim a share."

"What makes you so quiet?" asked Lloyd, as they rode on down the avenue.

"I was thinking of the way Joyce's fairy tale ended," said Betty. "'So the prince came into his kingdom, the kingdom of loving hearts and gentle hands.' Only this time it's the princess who's come into her kingdom."

"What do you mean?" asked Lloyd, with a puzzled look.

"Oh, it's only some of my foolishness," said Betty, looking back over her shoulder with a laugh. "I'm just so glad that I'm alive, and so glad that I am me, and so happy because everybody is so heavenly kind to me, that I wouldn't change places with the proudest princess that ever sat on a throne."

"Then come on, and let's race to the post-office," cried Lloyd, dashing off, with Hero bounding along beside her.

From the post-office they rode to The Beeches, where Allison was cooking something over the camp-fire, beside the tent on the lawn.

It proved to be candy, and she waved a sticky spoon in welcome. Mrs. Walton was in a hammock, near by, her mending basket beside her, and Kitty and Elise on the grass at her feet, watching the molasses bubble up in the kettle. Betty felt a little shy at first, for this was her first meeting with the General's wife, and she wished that the girls would not insist on having an immediate outline of the play. It had seemed very fine indeed to her when she read it aloud to herself, or repeated it to Lloyd. It had not seemed a very childish thing to her even when she read it to her godmother. But she shrank from Mrs. Walton's criticism. It was with many blushes that she began. Afterward she wondered why she should have been timid about it. Mrs. Walton applauded it so heartily, and entered into plans for making the entertainment a success as enthusiastically as any of the girls.

"I bid to be witch!" cried Kitty, when Betty had finished.

"I'd like to be the queen, if you don't care," said Allison, "for I am the largest, and I'd rather act with Rob than the other boys. But it doesn't make any difference. I'll be anything you want me to."

"That's the way Betty planned it," said Lloyd. "I'm to be the captive princess, and Keith will be my brother whom the witch changes into a dog. That's Hero, of co'se. Malcolm will be the knight who rescues me. Rob Moore will be king, and Elise the queen of the fairies, and Ranald the ogah."

"Ranald said last night that he wouldn't be in the play if he had to learn a lot of foolishness to speak, or if he couldn't be disguised so that nobody would know him," said Kitty. "He'll help any other way, fixing the stage and the red lights and all that, but the Captain has a dread of making himself appear ridiculous. Now *I* don't. I'd rather have the funny parts than the high and mighty ones."

"He might be Frog-eye-Fearsome," suggested Betty. "Then he wouldn't have anything to do but drag the prince and princess across the stage to the ogre's tower, and the costume could be so hideous that no one could tell whether a human or a hob-goblin was inside of it."

"Who'll buy all the balloons for the fairies, and make our spangled wings?" asked Elise. "Oh, I know," she cried, instantly answering her own question. "I'll tell Aunt Elise all about it, and I know that she'll help."

"How will you go all the way to the seashore to tell her?" asked Kitty.

"She isn't at the seashore," answered Elise, with an air of triumph. "She came back from Narragan-sett Pier last night. Didn't she, mamma? And she and Malcolm and Keith are coming out to grand-mother's this afternoon as straight as the train can carry them, you might know.   They always do, first thing. Don't they, mamma?"

Mrs. Walton nodded yes, then said: "Suppose you bring the play down this afternoon, Betty.   Ask your mother to come too, Lloyd, and we'll read it out under the trees.   Now are all the characters decided upon?"

"All but the ogre," said Betty.

"Joe Clark is the very one for that," exclaimed Lloyd.   "He is head and shouldahs tallah than all the othah boys, although he is only fifteen, and his voice is so deep and gruff it sounds as if it came out of the cellah.   We can stop and ask him if he'll take the part."

"Invite him to come down to the reading of the play, too," said Mrs. Walton.   "I'll look for you all promptly at four."

Betty almost lost her courage that afternoon when she saw the large group waiting for her under the beech-trees on Mrs. Walton's lawn.   Mrs. MacIntyre was there, fresh and dainty as Betty always remembered her, with the sunshine flickering softly through the leaves on her beautiful white hair.   Miss Allison, who, in the children's opinion, knew everything, sat beside her, and worst of all, the younger Mrs. Mac-Intyre was there; Malcolm's and Keith's mother, whom Betty had never seen before, but of whom she had heard glowing descriptions from her admiring sons.

Lloyd pointed her out to Betty as they drove in at the gate. "See, there she is, in that lovely pink organdy. Wouldn't you love to look like her? I would. She's like a queen."

Betty sank back, faint with embarrassment. "Oh, godmother!" she whispered. "I know I can't read it before all those people. It will choke me. There's at least a dozen, and some of them are strangers."

Mrs. Sherman smiled, encouragingly. "There's nothing to be afraid of, dear. Your play is beautiful, in my opinion, and every one there will agree with me when they've all heard it. Go on and do your best and make us all proud of you."

There was no time to hesitate. Keith was already swinging on the carriage steps to welcome them, and Malcolm and Ranald were bringing out more chairs to make places for them with the group under the beeches. Nobody mentioned the play for some time. The older people were busy questioning Mrs. Sherman about her summer abroad, and Malcolm and Keith had much to tell the others of their vacation at the seashore; of polo and parties and ping-pong, and several pranks that sent the children into shrieks of laughter.

In the midst of the hum of conversation Betty's heart almost stood still. Mrs. Walton was calling the company to order. Coming forward, she led Betty to a chair in the centre of the circle, and asked her to begin. It was with hands that trembled visibly that Betty opened her note-book and began to read "The Rescue of the Princess Winsome."

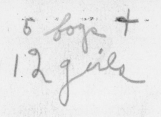

5 boys +
12 girls

CHAPTER XIII.

"THE RESCUE OF THE PRINCESS WINSOME"

AN ENTERTAINMENT FOR THE BENEFIT OF THE RED CROSS

CHARACTERS

King	Rob Moore.	
Queen	Allison Walton.	*Mary Louise*
Prince Hero . . .	Keith MacIntyre.	
PRINCESS WINSOME .	Lloyd Sherman.	*Josephine*
Knight	Malcolm MacIntyre.	
Ogre	Joe Clark.	*Leslie*
Witch	Kitty Walton.	*Mary & Jane*
Godmother . . .	Elizabeth Lloyd Lewis.	*& Peggy*
Frog-eye Fearsome . .	Ranald Walton.	
Titania	Elise Walton.	
Bewitched Prince . .	HERO, THE RED CROSS DOG.	
Chorus of Fairies.		

Flower Messengers . .
{
Morning-glory. *Nancy Jane*
Pansy. *Sarah Platt*
Rose. *Dorothy*
Forget-me-**not**. *Patrecia anny*
Poppy. *Marion*
Daisy. *Mary-alleine*
}

197

ACT I.

SCENE I. In the Witch's Orchard. Frog-eye Fearsome drags the captive Prince and Princess to the Ogre's tower. At Ogre's command Witch brews spell to change Prince Hero into a dog.

SCENE II. In front of Witch's Orchard. King and Queen bewail their loss. The Godmother of Princess promises aid. The Knight starts in quest of the South Wind's silver flute with which to summon the Fairies to his help.

ACT II.

SCENE I. In the Tower Room. PRINCESS WINSOME and HERO. Godmother brings spinning-wheel on which Princess is to spin Love's golden thread that shall rescue her brother. Dove comes with letter from Knight. Flower messengers in turn report his progress. Counting the Daisy's petals the Princess learns that her true Knight has found the flute.

ACT III.

SCENE I. In Witch's Orchard. Knight returns from quest. Blows the flute and summons Titania and her train. They bind the Ogre and Witch in the golden thread the Princess spun. Knight demands the spell that binds the Prince and plucks the seven golden plums from the silver apple-tree. Prince becomes a prince again, and King gives the Knight the hand of the Princess and half of his Kingdom. Chorus of Fairies.

ACT I.

SCENE I. *Witch bends over fire in middle of orchard, brewing a charm in her caldron. Ogre stalks in, grinning frightfully, swinging his bludgeon in triumph.*

Ogre. Ha, old witch, it is done at last!
I have broken the King's stronghold!
I have stolen away his children twain
From the clutch of their guardsmen bold.
I have dragged them here to my castle tower.
Prince Hero is strong and fair.
But he and his sister shall rue my power,
When once up yon winding stair.

Witch. Now why didst thou plot such a wicked thing?
The children no harm have done.

Ogre. But I have a grudge 'gainst their father, the King,
A grudge that is old as the sun.
And hark ye, old hag, I must have thy aid
Before the new moon be risen.
Now brew me a charm in thy caldron black,
That shall keep them fast in their prison!

Witch. I'll brew thee no charm, thou Ogre dread!
Knowest thou not full well
The Princess thou hast stolen away
Is guarded by Fairy spell?
Her godmother over her cradle bent.
"O Princess Winsome," she said,
" I give thee this gift: thou shalt deftly spin,
As thou wishest, Love's golden thread."
So I dare not brew thee a spell 'gainst her.
My caldron would grow acold

And never again would bubble up,
If touched by her thread of gold.

Ogre.   Then give me a charm to bind the prince.
Thou canst do that much at least.
I'll give thee more gold than hands can hold,
If thou'lt change him into some beast.

Witch.   I have need of gold — so on the fire
I'll pile my fagots higher and higher,
And in the bubbling water stir
This hank of hair, this patch of fur,
This feather and this flapping fin,
This claw, this bone, this dried snake skin!

Bubble and boil
And snake skin coil,
This charm shall all plans
But the Ogre's foil.

[*As Witch stirs and sings, the Ogre, stalking to the side, calls.*

Ogre.   Ho, Frog-eye Fearsome, let the sport begin!
Hence to the tower! Drag the captives in!

[*Frog-eye Fearsome drags Prince Hero and Princess Winsome across the stage, and into the door leading up the tower stair. They are bound by ropes. Prince tries to reach his sword. Princess shrieks.*

Princess.   Oh, save us, good, wise witch,
In pity, save us, pray.
The King, our royal father,
Thy goodness will repay.   [*Pulls back, wringing hand.*
Oh, I cannot, *cannot* mount the tower!
Oh, save us from the bloody Ogre's power!

[*They are dragged into the tower, door bangs and Ogre locks it with key a yard long. Goes back to Witch, who hands him vial filled from caldron with black mixture.*

Witch.   Pour drop by drop upon Prince Hero's tongue.

First he will bark.   His hands and feet
Will turn to paws, and he will seem a dog.
Seven drops will make the change complete.
The poison has no antidote save one,
And he a prince again can never be,
Unless seven silver plums he eats,
Plucked from my golden apple-tree.

   Ogre.   Revenge is sweet,
And soon 'twill be complete !
Then to my den I'll haste for gold to delve.
I'll bring it at the black, bleak hour of twelve !

   Witch.   And I upon my broomstick now must fly
To woodland tryst.   Come, Hornèd Owl
And Venomed Toad !   Now play the spy !
Let no one through my orchard prowl.

                              [Exit Witch and Ogre to dirge music.

SCENE II.   *Enter King and Queen weeping.   They pace up
    and down, wringing hands, and showing great signs of
    grief.   Godmother enters from opposite side.   King speaks.*

   King.   Good dame, Godmother of our daughter dear,
Perhaps thou'st heard our tale of woe.
Our children twain are stolen away
By Ogre Grim, mine ancient foe.

All up and down the land we've sought
For help to break into his tower.
And now, our searching all for nought,
We've come to beg the Witch's power.

    *[Godmother springs forward, finger to lip, and anxiously waves
        them away from orchard.*

   Godmother.   Nay ! Nay ! Your Majesty, go not
Within that orchard, now I pray !

The Witch and Ogre are in league.
They've wrought you fearful harm this day.
She brewed a draught to change the prince
Into a dog! Oh, woe is me!
I passed the tower and heard him bark:
Alack! That I must tell it thee!

> [*Queen shrieks and falls back in the King's arms, then recovering falls to wailing.*

    Queen. My noble son a *dog?* A *beast?*
It cannot, must not, *shall* not be!
I'll brave the Ogre in his den,
And plead upon my bended knee!

    Godmother. Thou couldst not touch his heart of stone.
He'd keep *thee* captive in his lair.
The Princess Winsome can alone
Remove the cause of thy despair.
And I unto the tower will climb,
And ere is gone the sunset's red,
Shall bid her spin a counter charm —
A skein of Love's own Golden Thread.
Take heart, O mother Queen! Be brave!
Take heart, O gracious King, I pray!
Well can she spin Love's Golden Thread,
And Love can *always* find a way!   [*Exit Godmother*

    Queen. She's gone, good dame. But what if she
Has made mistake, and thread of gold
Is not enough to draw our son
From out the Ogre's cruel hold?
Canst think of nought, your Majesty?
Of nothing else? Must we stand here
And powerless lift no hand to speed
The rescue of our children dear?

> [*King clasps hand to his head in thought, then starts forward.*

King. I have it now! This hour I'll send
Swift heralds through my wide domains,
To say the knight who rescues them
Shall wed the Princess for his pains.

Queen. Quick! Let us fly! I hear the sound of feet,
As if some horseman were approaching nigher.
'Twould not be seemly should he meet
Our royal selves so near the Witch's fire.

> [*They start to run, but are met by Knight on horseback in centre of
> stage. He dismounts and drops to one knee.*

King. 'Tis Feal the Faithful! Rise, Sir Knight,
And tell us what thou doest here!

Knight. O Sire, I know your children's plight.
I go to ease your royal fear.

Queen. Now if thou bringst them back to us,
A thousand blessings on thy head.

King. Ay, half my kingdom shall be thine.
The Princess Winsome thou shalt wed.

Queen. But tell us, how dost thou think to cope
With the Ogre so dread and grim?
What is the charm that bids thee hope
Thou canst rout and vanquish him?

Knight. My faithful heart is my only charm,
But my good broadsword is keen,
And love for the princess nerves my arm
With the strength of ten, I ween.
Come weal, come woe, no knight can fail
Who goes at Love's behest.
Long ere one moon shall wax and wane,
I shall be back from my quest.
I have only to find the South Wind's flute.
In the Land of Summer it lies.
It can awaken the echoes mute,

With answering replies.
And it can summon the fairy folk
Who never have said me nay.
They'll come to my aid at the flute's clear **call.**
Love *always* can find a way.

> *King.*   Go, Feal the Faithful.   It is **well!**
Successful mayst thou be,
And all the way that thou dost **ride,**
Our blessings follow thee.   **[*Curtain.*

ACT II.

SCENE. *Room in Ogre's tower.   Princess Winsome kneeling*
with arm around Dog's neck.

> *Princess.*   *Art* thou my brother?   Can **it be**
That thou hast taken such shape?
Oh turn those sad eyes not on me!
There *must* be some escape.
And yet our parents think us **dead.**
No doubt they weep this very **hour,**
For no one ever has escaped,
Ere this, the Ogre's power.

Oh cruel fate!   We can but **die!**
Each moment seems a week.
Is there no hope?   Oh, Hero **dear,**
If thou couldst only speak!
But no!   Within this tower **room**
We're captive, and despair
Must settle on us.   'Tis the doom
Of all dragged up yon winding stair.

> [*Drops her head and weeps.   Enter Godmother, who waves wand*
> *and throwing back curtain, displays a spinning-wheel.*

Godmother. Rise, Princess Winsome,
Dry your weeping eyes.
The way of escape
Within your own hand lies.

Waste no time in sorrow,
Spin and sing instead.
Spin 'for thy brother's sake,
A skein of golden thread.

Question not the future,
Mourn not the past,
But keep thy wheel a-turning,
Spinning well and fast.

All the world helps gladly
Those who help themselves,
And the thread thou spinnest,
Shall be woven by elves.

All good things shall speed thee!
Thy knight, the Faithful Feal,
Is to thy rescue riding.
Up! To thy spinning-wheel!   *[Disappears behind curtain*

Princess. All good things shall speed me?
Sir Knight, the Faithful Feal,
Is to my rescue riding?   *[In joyful surprise*
Turn, turn, my spinning-wheel!
(She sings.)

Spinning Wheel Song.

1. My god-mother bids me spin, that my heart may not be

sad. Spin and sing for my brother's sake, and the

Spinning Wheel Song. Continued.

spinning makes me glad.   2. Spin, sing with

humming whir, the wheel goes round and round. For my

brother's sake, the charm I'll break, Prince Hero shall be found.

Spinning Wheel Song.   Concluded.

Spin, sing, the golden thread, Gleams in the sun's bright ray, The

humming wheel my grief can heal, For love will find a way.

[Pauses with uplifted hand.

What's that at my casement tapping?

Some messenger, maybe.

Pause, good wheel, in thy turning,

While I look out and see.

[Opens casement and leans out, as if welcoming a carrier dove,
which may be concealed in basket outside window.

Little white dove, from my faithful knight,

Dost thou bring a message to me?

Little white dove with the white, white breast,

What may that message be?

[Finds note, tied to wing

Here is his letter. Ah, well-a-day!

I'll open it now, and read.

Little carrier dove, with fluttering heart,

I'm a happy maiden, indeed.

(*She reads.*) "O Princess fair, in the Ogre's tower,

In the far-off Summer-land

I seek the South Wind's silver flute,

To summon a fairy band.

Now send me a token by the dove

That thou hast read my note.

Send me the little heart of gold

From the chain about thy throat.

And I shall bind it upon my shield,

My talisman there to stay.

And then all foes to me must yield,

For Love will find the way.

Here is set the hand and seal

Of thy own true knight, the faithful — Feal."

[Princess takes locket from throat and winds chain around dove'.
neck.

Princess sings.

The Dove Song.

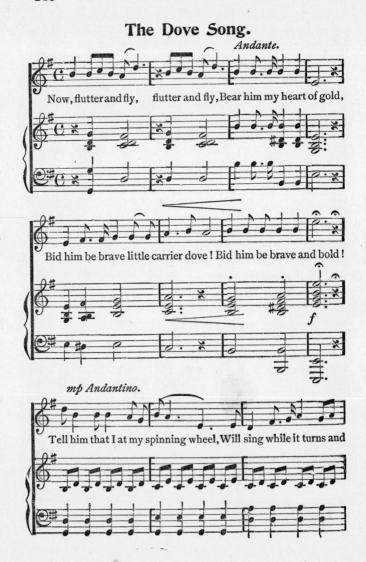

Andante.

Now, flutter and fly, flutter and fly, Bear him my heart of gold,

Bid him be brave little carrier dove! Bid him be brave and bold!

mp Andantino.

Tell him that I at my spinning wheel, Will sing while it turns and

The Dove Song. Concluded.

hums,   And think all day of his love so leal, Un-

til with the flute he comes.   Now fly,   flutter and

fly,   Now flutter and fly, a - way, a - way.

[Sets dove at liberty.   Turning to wheel again, repeats song.
Princess repeats.   My Godmother bids me spin,
That my heart may not be sad;
Spin and sing for my brother's sake,
And the spinning makes me glad.

Sing! Spin! With hum and whir
The wheel goes round and round.
For my brother's sake the charm I'll break!
Prince Hero shall be found.

Spin! Sing! The golden thread
Gleams in the sunlight's ray!
The humming wheel my grief can heal,
For Love will find a way.

[First messenger appears at window, dressed as a Morning-glory.
Morning-glory.   Fair Princess,
This morning, when the early dawn
Was flushing all the sky,
Beside the trellis where I bloomed,
A knight rode slowly by.

He stopped and plucked me from my stem,
And said, " Sweet Morning-glory,
Be thou my messenger to-day,
And carry back my story.

" Go bid the Princess in the tower
Forget all thought of sorrow.
Her true knight will return to her
With joy, on some glad morrow."   *[Disappears*

Princess sings.   Spin! spin! The golden thread
Holds no thought of sorrow,

My true knight he shall come to me
With joy on some glad morrow.
      [*Second flower messenger, dressed as Pansy, appears at window.*
  Pansy. Gracious Princess,
I come from Feal the Faithful.
He plucked me from my bower,
And said, speed to the Princess
And say, " Like this sweet flower
The thoughts within my bosom
Bloom ever, love, of thee.
Oh, read the pansy's message,
And give a thought to me."   [*Pansy disappears.*

   Princess sings. Spin, spin, O golden thread!
And turn, O humming wheel.
This pansy is his thought of me,
My true knight, brave and leal.
          [*Third flower messenger, a pink Rose.*
  Rose. Thy true knight battled for thee to-day,
On a fierce and bloody field,
But he won at last in the hot affray,
By the heart of gold on his shield.

He saw me blushing beside a wall,
My petals pink in the sun
With pleasure, because such a valiant knight
The hard-fought battle had won.

And he kissed me once on my soft pink cheek,
And once in my heart of gold,
And bade me hasten to thee and speak.
Pray take the message I hold.

[Princess goes to the window, takes a pink rose from the messenger. As she walks back, kisses it and fastens it on her dress. Then turns to wheel again.

Princess sings.   Spin, spin, O golden thread,
And turn, O happy wheel.
The pink rose brought in its heart of gold,
A kiss, his love to seal.

[Fourth messenger, a Forget-me-not.

Forget-me-not.   Fair Princess,
Down by the brook, when the sun was low,
A brave knight paused to slake
His thirst in the water's silver flow,
As he journeyed far for thy sake.
He saw me bending above the stream,
And he said, " Oh, happy spot !
Ye show me the Princess Winsome's eyes
In each blue forget-me-not."
He bade me bring you my name to hide
In your heart of hearts for ever,
And say as long as its blooms are blue,
No power true hearts can sever.

Princess sings.   Spin, spin, O golden thread.
O wheel, my happy lot
It is to hide within my heart
That name, forget-me-not.

[Fifth messenger, a Poppy.

Poppy.   Dear Princess Winsome,
Within the shade of a forest glade
He laid him down to sleep,
And I, the Poppy, kept faithful guard
That it might be sweet and deep.
But oft in his dreams he stirred and spoke,

And thy name was on his tongue,
And I learned his secret ere he woke,
When the fair new day was young.
And this is what he, whispering, said,
As he journeyed on in his way:
"Bear her my dreams in your chalice red,
For I dream of her night and day."

   Princess sings. Spin, spin, O golden thread.
He dreams of me night and day!
The poppy's chalice is sweet and red.
Oh, Love will find a way!
                        [*Sixth messenger, a Daisy.*

   Daisy. O Princess fair,
Far on the edge of the Summer-land
I stood with my face to the sun,
And the brave knight counted with strong hand
My petals, one by one.

And he said, " O Daisy, white and gold,
The princess must count them too.
By thy petals shall she be told
If my long, far quest is through.

"Whether or not her knight has found
The South Wind's flute that he sought."
So over the hills from the Summer-land,
Your true knight's token I've brought.
   [*Gives Princess a large artificial daisy. She counts petals, slowly
      dropping them one by one.*
   Princess. Far on the edge of the Summer-land,
O Daisy, white and gold,
My true love held you in his hand.
What was the word he told?

He's found it.   Found it not.
Found it.   Found it not.

That magic flute of the South Wind, **sweet,**
Will he blow it, over the lea?
Will the fairy folk its call repeat,
And hasten to rescue me?

He's found it, found it **not.**
Found it, found it **not.**
Found it, found it **not.**
He's *found* it!   [*Turning to the dog.*

Come, Hero!   Hear me, brother mine;
Thy gladness must indeed be mute,
But oh, the joy!   We're saved!   We're saved!
My knight has found the silver flute!

(*Sings.*)

"Spin, Wheel, Reel Out Thy Golden Thread."

"Spin, Wheel, Reel Out." Concluded.

hap - py heart sings glad and gay, Hero shall 'scape the

O - gre dread, And I my own true love shall wed. For

love has found a way, For love has found a way.

[Curtain.

ACT III.

SCENE. *In front of Witch's Orchard. Knight comes riding by, blows flute softly under the tower window. Princess leans out and waves her hand. Knight dismounts, and little page takes horse, leading it off stage.*

Knight.   Lean out of thy window, O Princess fair,
Rescuers now are at hand.
Thou shalt be led down the winding stair
By the Queen of the Fairy band.

Listen, as low on the South Wind's flute
I call the elves to our tryst.
Down rainbow bubbles they softly float,
Light-winged as stars in a mist.

> [*He blows on flute, and from every direction the Fairies come floating in, their gauzy wings spangled, and each one carrying a toy balloon, attached to a string. They trip back and forth, their balloons bobbing up and down like rainbow bubbles, singing.*

Fairy Chorus.

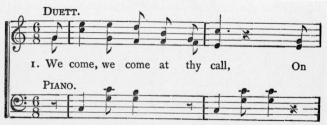

1. We come, we come at thy call,   On

Fairy Chorus. Continued.

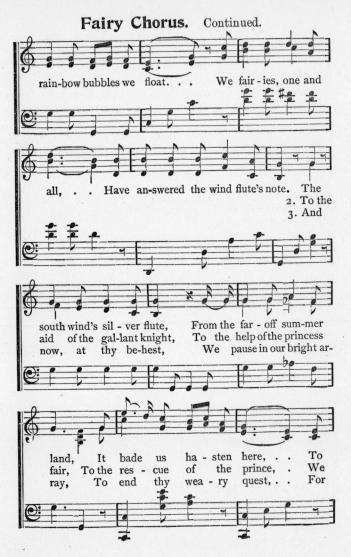

rain-bow bubbles we float. . . We fair-ies, one and

all, . . Have an-swered the wind flute's note. The
2. To the
3. And

south wind's sil-ver flute, From the far-off sum-mer
aid of the gal-lant knight, To the help of the princess
now, at thy be-hest, We pause in our bright ar-

land, It bade us ha-sten here, . . To
fair, To the res-cue of the prince, . We
ray, To end thy wea-ry quest, . . For

Fairy Chorus. Concluded.

lend   a   help - ing hand.   It bade   us   ha - sten,
come to the O - gre's lair.   To   the   res - cue
love has found   a   way.   To end   thy   wea - ry,

ha - sten here, To   lend   a   help - ing hand.
of   the   prince, We come to the   O - gre's   lair.
wea - ry   quest, For   love   has found   a   way.

[*Queen Titania coming forward, waves her star-tipped wand,
and looks up toward Princess at the window.*

Titania.   Princess Winsome,
When thy good Godmother
Bade thee spin Love's thread,
It was with this promise,
These the words she said:

All the world helps gladly
Those who help themselves.
The thread thou spinnest bravely,
Shall be woven by elves.

And now, O Princess Winsome,
How much hast thou spun,
As thy wheel, a-whirling,
Turned from sun to sun?

Princess. This, O Queen Titania.

[Holding up mammoth ball.

To the humming wheel's refrain,
I sang, and spun the measure
Of one great golden skein.

And winding, winding, winding,
At last I wound it all,
Until the thread all golden
Made a mammoth wonder-ball.

Titania. Here below thy casement
Thy true knight waiting stands.
Drop the ball thou holdest
Into his faithful hands.

*[Princess drops the ball, Knight catches it, and as Titania waves
her wand, he starts along the line of Fairies. They each take
hold as the Witch and Ogre come darting in, she brandish-
ing her broomstick, he his bludgeon. They come through
gate of the Orchard in the background. As the ball unwinds,
the Fairies march around them, tangling them in the yards
and yards of narrow yellow ribbon, singing as they go.*

Fairy Chorus. We come, we come at thy call,
On rainbow bubbles we float.
We fairies, one and all,
Have answered the Wind-flute's note.
To the aid of the gallant Knight,
To the help of the Princess fair,
To the rescue of the Prince,
We come to the Ogre's lair.

We come, we come at thy call,
The Witch and Ogre to quell,
And now they both must bow
To the might of the fairies' spell.
Love's Golden Thread can bind
The strongest Ogre's arm,
And the spell of the blackest Witch
Must yield to its mighty charm.

> [*Ogre and Witch stand bound and helpless, tangled in golden cord.
> They glower around with frightful grimaces. King and
> Queen enter unnoticed from side. Knight draws his sword,
> and brandishing it before Ogre, cries out fiercely.*

Knight.   The key!   The key that opens yonder tower!
Now give it me, or by my troth
Your head shall from your shoulders fly!
To stab you through I'm nothing loath!

> [*Ogre gives Knight the key. He rushes to the door, unlocks it,
> and Princess and dog burst out. Queen rushes forward and
> embraces her, then the King, and Knight kneels and kisses
> her hand. Princess turns to Titania.*

Princess.   Oh, happy day that sets me free
From yon dread Ogre's prison!
Oh, happy world, since 'tis for me
Such rescuers have 'risen.
But see, your Majesty! the plight
Of Hero — he the Prince, my brother!
Wilt thou *his* wrong not set aright?
Another favour grant!   One other!

> *Titania waves wand toward Knight who springs at Witch with
> drawn sword.*

Knight.   The spell!   The spell that breaks the power
That holds Prince Hero in its thrall!

Now give it me, or in this hour
Thy head shall from ⸺ shoulders fall!
    Witch.   Pluck with your thumbs
Seven silver plums   *[Speaking in high, cracked voice.*
From my golden apple-tree!
These the dog must eat.
The change will be complete,
And a prince once more the dog will be!

    *[Princess darts back into Orchard, followed by dog, who crouches
        behind hedge, and is seen no more. She picks plums, and,
        stooping, gives them to him, under cover of the hedge. The
        real Prince Hero leaps up from the place where he has been
        lying, waiting, and hand in hand they run back to the centre
        of the stage, where the Prince receives the embraces of King
        and Queen. Prince then turns to Knight.*

   Prince Hero.   Hail, Feal the Faithful!
My gratitude I cannot tell,
That thou at last hath freed me
From the Witch's fearful spell.
But wheresoe'er thou goest,
Thou faithful knight and true,
The favours of my kingdom
Shall all be showered on you.   *[Turns to Titania.*
Hail, starry-winged Titania!
And ye fairies, rainbow-hued!
I have not words sufficient
To tell my gratitude,
But if the loyal service
Of a mortal ye should need,
Prince Hero lives to serve you,
No matter what the deed!

    *[Characters now group themselves in tableau. Queen and Prince
        on one side, Godmother and Titania on the other. King in*

centre, with Princess on one hand, Knight on other. He
places her hand in the Knight's, who kneels to receive it. Ogre
and Witch, still making horrible faces, are slightly in back-
ground, bound. Fairies form an outer semicircle.

   King. And now, brave Knight, requited stand!
Here is the Princess Winsome's hand.
To-morrow thou shalt wedded be,
And half my kingdom is for thee!
   Fairy Chorus. Love's golden cord has bound
The strongest Ogre's arm,
And the spell of the blackest Witch
Has yielded to its charm.
The Princess Winsome plights —
Her troth to the Knight to-day,
So fairies, one and all,
We need no longer stay.

The golden thread is spun,
The Knight has won his bride,
And now our task is done,
We may no longer bide.
On rainbow bubbles bright,
We fairies float away.
The wrong is now set right
And Love has found the way!

                                              [*Curtain.*

As Betty finished reading, there was a babel of
voices and a clapping of hands that made her face
grow redder and redder. They were all trying to
congratulate her at once, and she was so confused
that she wished she could run away and hide. But

the applause was very sweet to shy little Betty. She felt that she had done her best, and that not only her godmother was proud of her, but Keith, and Keith's beautiful mother, who bent from her queenly height to kiss Betty's flushed cheek, and whisper a word of praise that made her glow for weeks afterward, whenever she thought of it.

"'And he kissed me once on my soft pink cheek,
  And once in my heart of gold,'"

hummed Keith. "Say, Betty, that's mighty pretty. How did you ever think of it?"

Before she could answer, one of the maids came out with a tray of sherbet and cake, and the boys sprang up to help serve the girls.

"I know some of my part already," said Kitty, stirring her sherbet suggestively, and repeating in a sepulchral tone:

"'I'll stir
  This hank of hair, this patch of fur,
  This feather and this flapping fin,
  This claw, this bone, this dried snake skin.'"

"Oh, Kitty, for mercy's sake _hush!_" said Allison; "you make my blood run cold."

"But I must, if we've only a week to get ready in. I expect to say it day and night. It's better to do that than to take more than a week, and give up the camping party, isn't it?"

"It's going to be a howling success," prophesied Malcolm. "When mamma and auntie and Aunt Mary go into a scheme the way they are doing now, costumes and drills, and all sorts of impossible things don't count at all. We'll be ready in plenty of time."

"Especially," said the Little Colonel, with dignity, "when mothah and Papa Jack are goin' to do so much. My pa'ht is longah than anybody's."

Next morning at the depot, the post-office, and the blacksmith shop a sign was displayed which everybody stopped to read. Similar announcements nailed on various trees throughout the Valley caused many an old farmer to pull up his team and adjust his spectacles for a closer view of this novel poster.

They were all Miss Allison's work. Each one bore at the top a crayon sketch of a huge St. Bernard, with a Red Cross on its collar and shoulder-bags. Underneath was a notice to the effect that an entertainment would be given the following Friday night in the college hall, a short concert, followed by a play called "The Princess Winsome's Rescue," in which *Hero*, the Red Cross dog recently brought from Switzerland, would take a prominent part. The proceeds were to be given to the cause of the Red Cross.

That announcement alone would have drawn a large crowd, but added to that was the fact that twenty families in the Valley had each contributed a child to the fairy chorus or the group of flower messengers, and were thus personally interested in the success of the entertainment.

There was scarcely standing-room when the doors were opened Friday evening. Papa Jack felt well repaid for his part in the hurried preparations when, after the musical part of the programme, he heard the buzz of admiration that went around the room, as the curtain rose on the first scene of the play It was the dimly lighted witch's orchard.

Across the stage, five feet back from the footlights, ran a snaky-looking fence with high-spiked posts. It had taken him all morning to build it, even with Alec's and Walker's help. Above this peered a thicket of small trees and underbrush bearing a marvellous crop of gold and silver apples and plums. Real gold and silver fruit it looked to be in the dim light, and not the discarded ornaments of a score of old Christmas-trees. A stuffed owl kept guard on one high gate-post, and a huge black velvet cat on the other.

In the centre of the stage, showing plainly through the open double gates, the witch's caldron hung on a tripod, over a fire of fagots. Here Kitty, dressed like an old hag, leaned on her blackened broomstick, stirring the brew, and muttering to herself.

At one side of the stage could be seen the door leading into the ogre's tower, and above it a tiny casement window.

Mrs. Walton gave a nod of satisfaction over her work, when the ogre came roaring in. His costume was of her making, even to the bludgeon which he carried. "Nobody could guess that it was only an old Indian club painted red to hide the lumps of sealing-wax I had to stick on to make the regulation knots," she whispered to Keith's father, who sat next her. "And no one would ever dream that the ogre is Joe Clark. I had hard work to persuade him to take the part, but an invitation to my camping party next week proved to be effective bait. And such a time as I had to get Ranald's costume! I was about to ask Betty to change his name, when Elise found that Mardi Gras frog at some costumer's. Those webbed feet and hideous eyes are enough to strike terror to any one's soul."

It was a play in which every one was pleased with the part given him. Allison and Rob swept up and down in their gilt crowns and ermine-trimmed robes of royal purple, feeling that as king and queen they had the most important parts of all. Keith looked every inch the charming Prince Hero he personated, and Malcolm made such a dashing knight that there was a burst of applause every time he appeared.

Betty made a dear old godmother, and Elise, with crown and star-tipped wand, filmy spangled wings, and big red bubble of a balloon, was supremely happy as Queen of the Fairies. But it was the Little Colonel who won the greatest laurels, in the tower room, making the prettiest picture of all as she bent over the great St. Bernard, bewailing their fate.

The scenery had been changed with little delay between acts. Three tall screens, hastily unfolded just in front of the spiked fence, hid the orchard from view, and a fourth screen served the double purpose of forming the side wall of the room, and hiding the ogre's tower. The narrow space between the screens and the footlights was ample for the scene that took place there, and the arrangement saved much trouble. For in the last act, the screens had only to be carried away, to leave the stage with its original setting.

"Lloyd never looked so pretty before, in her life,"

said Mr. Sherman to his wife, as they watched the Princess Winsome tread back and forth beside the spinning-wheel, the golden cord held lightly in her white fingers.   But she was even prettier in the next scene, when with the dove in her hands she stood at the window, twining the slender gold chain about its neck and singing in a high, sweet voice, clear as a crystal bell :

> " Flutter and fly, flutter and fly,
>   Bear him my heart of gold.
>   Bid him be brave, little carrier dove,
>   Bid him be brave and bold."

Twice many hands called her back, and many eyes looked admiringly as she sang the song again, holding the dove to her breast and smoothing its white feathers as she repeated the words :

> " Tell him that I at my spinning-wheel
>   Will sing while it turns and hums,
>   And think all day of his love so leal
>   Until with the flute he comes."

" Jack," said some one in a low tone to Mr. Sherman, as the applause died away for the third time, " Jack, when the Princess Winsome is a little older, you'd be wise to call in the ogre's help.   You'll have more than one Kentucky Knight trying to carry her away if you don't."

"'SPIN, WHEEL, REEL OUT THY GOLDEN THREAD'"

Mr. Sherman made some laughing reply, but turned away so absorbed by a thought that his friend's words had suggested that he lost all of the flower messengers' speeches. That some knight might want to carry off his little Princess Winsome was a thought that had never occurred to him except as some remote possibility far in the future. But looking at her as she stood in her long court train, he realised that in a few more months she would be in her teens, and then — time goes so fast! He sighed, thinking with a heavy sinking of the heart that it might be only a few years until she would be counting the daisy petals in earnest.

The curtain hitched just at the last, so that it would not go down, so with their rainbow bubbles bright the fairies ran off the stage toward various points in the audience, for the coveted admiration and praise which they knew was their due.

"Wasn't Hero fine? Didn't he do his part beautifully?" cried Lloyd, as her father, with one long step, raised himself up to a place beside her on the stage, where the children were holding an informal reception.

"Show him the money-box," cried Keith, pressing down through the crowds from the outer door whither he had gone after the entrance receipts.

"Just look, old fellow. There's dollars and dollars in there. See what you've done for the Red Cross. If it hadn't been for you, Betty never would have written the play."

"And if it hadn't been for Betty's writing the play you never would have sent me this heart of gold," said Malcolm in an aside to Lloyd, as he unfastened her locket and chain from his shield. "Am I to keep it always, fair princess?"

"No, indeed!" she answered, laughingly, holding out her hand to take it. "Papa Jack gave me that, and I wouldn't give it up to any knight undah the sun."

"That's right, little daughter," whispered her father. "I am not in such a hurry to give up my Princess Winsome as the old king was. Come, dear, help me find Betty. I want to tell her what a grand success it was."

Lloyd slipped a hand in her father's and led him toward a wing whither the shy little godmother had fled, without a glance in Malcolm's direction. But afterward, when she came out of the dressing-room, wrapped in her long party-cloak, she saw him standing by the door. "Good night!" he said, waving his plumed helmet. Then, with a mischievous smile, he sang in an undertone:

" Go bid the princess in the tower
   Forget all thought of sorrow.
   Her true knight will return to her
   With joy, on some glad morrow."

CHAPTER XIV.

IN CAMP

SEVERAL miles from Lloydsboro Valley, where a rapid brook runs by the ruins of an old paper-mill, a roaring waterfall foams and splashes. Even in the long droughts of midsummer it is green and cool there, for the spray, breaking on the slippery stones, freshens the ferns on the bank, and turns its moss to the vivid hue of an emerald. Near by, in an open pasture, sloping down from a circle of wooded hills, lies an ideal spot for a small camp.

It was here that Mrs. Walton and Miss Allison came one warm afternoon, the Monday following the entertainment, with a wagonette full of children. Ranald, Malcolm, Keith, and Rob Moore had ridden over earlier in the day to superintend the coloured men who dug the trenches and pitched the tents. By the time the wagonette arrived, fuel enough to last a week was piled near the stones where the camp-fire was laid, and everything was in readiness for the gay party. Flags floated from the tent poles, and Dinah, the young coloured woman who was to be the cook, came up from the spring, balancing a pail of water on her head, smiling broadly.

As the boys and girls swarmed out and scurried away in every direction like a horde of busy ants, Mrs. Walton turned to her sister with a laugh. "Did we lose any of them on the way, Allison? We'd better count noses."

"No, we are all here: eight girls, four boys, the four already on the field, Dinah and her baby, and ourselves, twenty in all."

"Twenty-one, counting Hero," corrected Mrs. Walton, as the great St. Bernard went leaping after Lloyd, sniffing at the tents, and barking occasionally to express his interest in the frolic. "He seems to be enjoying it as much as any of us."

"I wish that they were all as able to take care of themselves as he is. It would save us a world of anxiety. Do you begin to realise, Mary, what a load of responsibility we have taken on our shoulders? Sixteen boys and girls to keep out of harm's way for a week in the woods is no easy matter."

"We'll keep them so busy that they'll have no time for mischief. The wagonette isn't unloaded yet. Wait till you see the games I've brought, and the fishing-tackle. There's an old curtain that can be hung between those two trees any time we want to play charades."

"Swing that hammock over there, Ranald," she called, nodding to a clump of trees near the spring. "Then some of you boys can carry this chest back to Dinah." She pointed to the old army mess-chest, that always accompanied them on their picnics and outings.

"The Ogre can do that," said the Little Captain, nodding toward Joe Clark, who stood leaning lazily against a tree.

"Do it yourself, Frog-Eye Fearsome," retorted Joe, at the same time coming forward to help carry the chest to the place assigned it.

"They'll never be able to get away from those names," said Miss Allison. "Well, what is it, my Princess Winsome?" she asked, as Lloyd came running up to her.

"Please take care of these for me, Miss Allison," answered Lloyd, holding out Hero's shoulder-bags, which she had just taken from him. "I put on his things when we started, for mothah says nobody evah knows what's goin' to happen in camp, and we might need those bandages." Tumbling them into Miss Allison's lap, she was off again in breathless haste, to follow the other girls, who were exploring the tents, and exclaiming over all the queer make-shifts of camp life. Then they raced down to the waterfall, and, taking off shoes and stockings, waded up and down in the brook. These early fall days were as warm as August, so wading was not yet one of the forbidden pastimes. They splashed up and down until the Little Captain's bugle sent a ringing call for their return to camp. Katie was one of the last to leave the water. Lloyd waited for her while she hurriedly laced her shoes, and as they followed the others she said, in a confidential tone, "Do you think you are goin' to like to stay out heah till next Sata'day ?"

"Like it !" echoed Katie, "I could stay here a year !"

"But at night, I mean. Sleepin' in those narrow little cots, with nothin' ovah ou' heads but the tents, and no floah. Ugh! What if a snake or a liz'ad should wiggle in, and you'd heah it rustlin' around in the grass undah you! There's suah to be bugs and ants and cattahpillahs. I like camp in the day-light, but it would be moah comfortable to have a house to sleep in at night. I wish I could wish myself back home till mawnin'."

"I don't mind the bugs and spiders," said Katie,

recklessly, "and you'd better not let the boys find out that you do, or they'll never stop teasing you."

A bountifully spread supper-table met their sight as they reached the camp. It had been made by laying long boards across two poles, which were supported by forked stakes driven into the ground. The eight girls made a rush for the camp-stools on one side of the table, and the eight boys grabbed those on the other side.

"Don't have to have no manners in the woods," remarked little Freddy Nicholls, straddling his stool, and beginning his supper, regardless of the knife and fork beside his plate. "That's what I like about camping out. You don't have to wait to have things handed to you, but can dip in and get what you want like an Injun."

Lloyd looked at him scornfully as she daintily unfolded her paper napkin. She nodded a decided yes when Katie whispered, "Aren't boys horrid and greedy!" Then she corrected herself hastily. She had seen Malcolm wait to pass a dish of fried chicken to his Aunt Allison before helping himself, and heard Ranald apologise to his next neighbour for accidentally jogging his elbow. "Not all of them," she replied.

It added much to Betty's interest in the meal to

know that the cup from which she drank, and the fork with which she ate, had been used by real soldiers, and carried from one army post to another many times in the travel-worn old mess chest.

Little Elise was the only one who did not give due attention to her supper. She sat with a cooky in her hand, looking off at the hills with dreamy eyes, until her mother spoke to her.

"I am trying to make some poetry like Betty did," she answered. Ever since the play her thoughts seemed trying to twist themselves into rhymes, and she was constantly coming up to her mother with a new verse she had just made.

"Well, what is it, Titania?" asked Mrs. Walton, seeing from the gleam of satisfaction in the black eyes that the verse was ready.

"It's all of our names," she said, shyly, waving her hand toward the girls on her side of the table.

"Betty, Corinne, and Lloyd, Margery, Kitty, and Kate,
Allison and Elise all together make eight."

"Oh, that's easy," said Rob. "You just strung a lot of names together. Anybody can do that."

"You do it, then," proposed Kitty. "Make a verse with the boys' names in it."

"Malcolm, Ranald, and Rob, Jamie, Freddy,

Keith," he began, boldly, then hesitated. "There isn't any rhyme for Keith."

"Change them around," suggested Malcolm. The girls would not help, and the whole row of boys floundered among the names for a while, unwilling to be beaten by the youngest member of the party, and a girl, at that. Finally, by their united efforts and a hint from Miss Allison, they succeeded.

" Malcolm, Ranald, and Rob, Keith and Freddy, and James,
Joe the Ogre, and George. Those are the boys' eight names."

"Let's make a law," suggested Kitty, "that nobody at the table can say anything from now on till we are through supper, unless they speak in rhymes."

They all agreed, but for a few minutes no one ventured a remark. Only giggles broke the silence, until Allison asked Freddy Nicholls to pass the pickles. Recorded here in a book, it may seem a very silly game, but to the jolly camping party, ready to laugh at even the sheerest nonsense, it proved to be the source of much fun. Even Freddy, to his own great delight, surprised himself and the company by asking Elise to take some cheese. Joe was thrown into confusion by Kitty's asking him if flesh, fowl, or fish, was his favourite dish. As he could only nod his head, he had to pay a forfeit, and Keith answered for him by saying, " That's not a fair question to Joe. An ogre eats all things, you know." So it went on until Mrs. Walton said :

" Now all who are able, may rise from the table.
    The camp-fire's burning bright.
Spread rugs on the ground, and gather around,
    And we'll all tell tales in its light."

" This is the jolliest part of it all ! " exclaimed Keith, a little later, as; stretched out on a thick Indian blanket, he looked around on the circle of faces, glowing in the light of the leaping fagot-fire. Twilight had settled on the camp. The tumbling of the waterfall over the rocks made a subdued roar in the background. An owl called somewhere from the depths of the woods. As the dismal " Tu-whit, tu who-oo " sounded through the gloaming, Lloyd glanced over her shoulder with a shudder.

" Ugh ! " she exclaimed. " It looks as if the witch's orchard might be there behind us, with all sorts of snaky, crawlin' things in it. Come heah, Hero. Let me put my back against you. It makes me feel shivery to even think of such a thing ! "

The dog edged nearer at her call, and she snuggled up against his tawny curls with a feeling of warmth and protection.

" Wish I had a dog like that," said Jamie, fondly

stroking the silky ear that was nearest him. "I wouldn't take a thousand dollars for him if I had."

"Money couldn't buy Hero!" exclaimed Lloyd.

"Now what would you do," said Kitty, who was always supposing impossible things, "if some old witch would come to you and say, 'You may have your choice; a palace full of gold and silver and precious stones and give up Hero, or keep him and be a beggar in rags?'"

"I'd be a beggah, of co'se!" cried Lloyd, warmly, throwing her arm around the dog's neck. "Think I'd go back on anybody that had saved my life? But I wouldn't stay a beggah," she continued. "I'd put on the Red Cross too, and we'd go away where there was war, Hero and I, and we'd spend ou' lives takin' care of the soldiahs. I wouldn't have to dress in rags, for I'd weah the nurse's costume, and I'd do so much good that some day, may be, somebody would send me the Gold Cross of Remembrance, as they did Clara Barton, and I'm suah that I'd rathah have that, with all it means, than all the precious stones and things that the witch could give me."

"When did Hero save your life?" asked Joe, who had not heard the story of the runaway in Geneva.

"Tell us all about it, Lloyd," asked Mrs. Walton.

"THE CLEAR CALL . . . RANG OUT INTO THE DARK
WOODS"

So Lloyd began, and the group around the fire listened with breathless attention. And that was followed by the Major's story, and all he had told her of St. Bernard dogs, and of the Red Cross service. Then the finding of the Major by his faithful dog on the dark mountain after the storm. Betty's turn came next. She repeated some of the stories they had heard on shipboard. Mrs. Walton added her part afterward, telling her personal experience with the Red Cross work in Cuba and the Philippines.

"That is one reason I took such a deep interest in your little entertainment," she said, "and was so pleased when it brought so much money. I know that every penny under the wise direction of the Red Cross will help to make some poor soldier more comfortable; or if some sudden calamity should come in this country, before it was sent away, your little fund might help to save dozens of lives."

The fire had burned low while they talked, and Elise was yawning sleepily. Miss Allison looked at her watch. "How the time has flown!" she exclaimed in surprise. "Where is the bugler of this camp? It is high time for him to play taps."

Ranald ran for his bugle, and the clear call that he had learned to play when he was "The Little Captain," in far-away Luzon, rang out into the dark woods. It was answered by the same silvery notes. Mrs. Walton and Miss Allison looked at each other in surprise, for the reply was no echo, but the call of a real bugle, somewhere not far away.

"Oh, we forgot to tell you, Aunt Mary," said Malcolm, noting the surprised glance. "It's a regiment of the State Guard, in camp over by Calkin's Cliff. We boys were over there this morning. They made a big fuss over us when they found that Ranald was General Walton's son and we were his nephews. They wanted us to stay to dinner, and when they found out that you were coming to camp here, the Colonel said he wanted to come over here and call. He used to know you out West."

"Colonel Wayne," repeated Mrs. Walton, when Malcolm finally remembered the name. "We knew him when he was only a young cadet at West Point. The General was very fond of him, and I shall be glad to see him again."

"They'll be interested in Hero," said Ranald. "Maybe they'll want to train some war dogs for our army if they see him at work. Do you suppose he has forgotten his training, Lloyd? Let's try him in the morning."

"You can make a great game of it," suggested Mrs. Walton. "Rig up one of the tents for a hospital. Some of the boys can be wounded soldiers and some of the girls nurses."

"All but me," said Lloyd. "I'll have to be an officer to give the ordahs. He only knows the French words for that, and the Majah taught them to me."

"What can we use for the brassards and costumes?" said Kitty.

"Elise has an old red apron in the clothes-hamper that we can cut up for crosses," said Mrs. Walton, always ready for emergencies. "But now to your tents, every man of you, or you'll never be ready to get up in the morning."

It was hard to go to sleep in the midst of such strange surroundings, and more than once Lloyd started up, aroused by the hoot of an owl, or the thud of a bat against the side of the tent. Not until she reached out and laid her hand on the great St. Bernard stretched out beside her cot, did she settle herself comfortably to sleep. With the touch of his soft curls against her fingers, she was no longer afraid.

When the officers came into the camp next day, they found the children in the midst of their new game. It was some time before their attention was attracted to it, for the Colonel was one of the men

who had followed General Walton on his long, hard
Indian campaign, and there were many questions to
be asked and answered about mutual friends in the
army.

Hero was not making a serious business of the
game, but was entering into it as if it were a big
frolic. He could not make believe as the boys
could, who played at soldiering. But the old words
of command, uttered in the Little Colonel's high, excited voice, sent him bounding in the direction she
pointed, and the prostrate forms he found scattered
about the sham battle-field, seemed to quicken his
memory. Mrs. Walton presently called the officer's
attention to the efforts Hero was making to recall
his old lessons, and briefly outlined his history.

"I believe he would remember perfectly," said the
Colonel, watching him with deep interest, "if we
were to take him over to our camp, and try him
among the regular uniformed soldiers. Of course
our accoutrements are not the kind he has been accustomed to, but I think they would suggest them.
At least the smell of powder would be familiar, and
the guns and canteens and knapsacks might awaken
something in his memory that would revive his entire
training. I should like very much to make the
experiment."

After some further conversation, Lloyd was called up to meet the officers, and it was agreed that Hero should be taken over to the camp for a trial on the day the sham battle was to take place.

"The day has not yet been definitely determined," said the Colonel, "but I'll send you word as soon as it is. By the way, my orderly was once a young French officer, and often talks of the French army. He'll welcome Hero like a long-lost brother, for he has a soft spot in his heart for anything connected with his motherland. I'll send him over either this evening or to-morrow."

That evening the orderly rode over to bring word that the sham battle would take place the following Thursday, and they were all invited to witness it. Hero's trial would take place immediately after the battle. While he stood talking to Mrs. Walton and Miss Allison, Lloyd and Kitty came running down the hill with Hero close behind them.

The orderly turned with an exclamation of admiration as the dog came toward him, and held out his hand with a friendly snap of the fingers. "Ah, old comrade," he called out in French, in a deep, hearty voice. "Come, give me a greeting! I, too, am from the motherland."

At sound of the familiar speech, the dog went forward, wagging his tail violently, as if he recognised an old acquaintance. Then he stopped and snuffed his boots in a puzzled manner, and looked up wistfully into the orderly's face. It was a stranger he gazed at, yet voice, speech, and appearance were like the man's who had trained him from a puppy, and he gave a wriggle of pleasure when the big hand came down on his head, and the deep voice spoke caressingly to him.

When the orderly mounted his horse, Hero would have followed had not the Little Colonel called him sharply, grieved and jealous that he should show such marked interest in a stranger. He turned back at her call, but stood in the road, looking after his new-found friend, till horse and rider disappeared down the bridle-path that led through the deep woods to the other camp.

CHAPTER XV.

THE SENTRY'S MISTAKE

PROMPTLY on Thursday, at the time appointed, the orderly rode over to Camp Walton to escort the party back to the camp at Calkin's Cliff. The four boys led the way on their ponies; the rest piled into a great farm wagon filled with straw, that had been procured from one of the neighbouring farms for the occasion.

Hero followed obediently, when the Little Colonel ordered him to jump up beside her, but he turned longing eyes on the orderly, whom he had welcomed with strong marks of pleasure. It was only their second meeting, but Hero seemed to regard him as an old friend. He leaped up to lick his face, and bounded around him with quick, short barks of pleasure that, for the moment, gave Lloyd a jealous pang. She was hurt that Hero should show such an evident desire to follow him in preference to her.

"I don't see what makes Hero act so," she said to Mrs. Walton.

"The orderly certainly must bear a strong resemblance to some one whom Hero knew and loved in France," she replied. "You have owned him less than two months, and he has been away from France only a year, you must remember. Everything must seem strange to him here. He was not brought up to play with children, as many St. Bernards are.

"The other night, at the entertainment, I wondered many times what Hero must think of his strange surroundings. His life here is different in every way from all that he has been used to. A dog trained from puppyhood to the experiences of soldier life would naturally miss the excitement of camp as much as a soldier suddenly retired to the life ot a private citizen."

"Oh, deah!" sighed Lloyd, "I wish he could talk. I'd ask him if he is unhappy. *Are* you homesick, old fellow?"

She took his great head between her little hands and looked earnestly into his eyes as she asked the question.

"*Do* you wish you were back in the French army, following the ambulances and hunting the wounded soldiahs? Seems to me you ought to like it so much bettah heah in Kentucky, with nothing to do

but play and eat and sleep, and be loved by everybody."

"But an army dog can't get away from his training any easier than a man," laughed the orderly, as
he rode on beside the wagon. "It is a part of him.
Hero is a good soldier, and no doubt feels a greater
joy in obeying what he considers a call to duty, than
in riding in the wagon at his ease, with the ladies."

"You know a great deal, perhaps, of this society
for the training of ambulance dogs," said Mrs.
Walton.

"Yes," he replied. "I am deeply interested in
it. My brother at home keeps me informed of its
movements, and has written me much of Herr
Bungartz's methods. I think I shall have no diffi-
culty in putting the dog through his manœuvres,
especially as he seems to recognise me and in some
way connect me with his past life."

Fife and drum welcomed the party as they drove
into camp, and the party were at once escorted to
seats where they could watch the drill and the sham
battle. It was a familiar scene to the General's
little family, and to Miss Allison, who had visited
more than one army post. But some of the girls
put their fingers in their ears when the noise of the
rapid firing began. Hero was greatly excited.

Soon after the noise of the sham battle ceased, the field was prepared for the dog's trial. Men were hidden behind logs, stretched out in ditches, and left lying as if dead, in the dense thicket that skirted one side of the field, for wounded animals, either men or beasts, instinctively crawl away to die under cover.

With hands almost trembling in their eagerness, Lloyd fastened the flask and shoulder-bags on the dog. He seemed to know that something unusual was expected of him, and wagged his tail so violently that he nearly upset the Little Colonel. He watched every movement of the orderly, who, with a Red Cross brassard on his arm, was acting as chief of the improvised ambulance corps.

"Will you give him the order, Miss Lloyd?" he asked, turning politely to the little girl. Lloyd had pictured this moment several times on the way over, thinking how proud she would be to stand up like a real Little Colonel and send her orders ringing over the field before the whole admiring regiment. But now that the moment had actually come, she blushed and shrank back timidly. She was not sure that she could say the strange French words just as the Major had taught them to her, when such a crowd of soldiers were standing by to hear.

"Oh, *you* do it, please," she asked.

"If you will tell me the exact words he has been accustomed to hearing," answered the orderly.

Lloyd stammered them out, greatly embarrassed, feeling that her pronunciation must have grown quite faulty from lack of practice under the Major's careful training. The orderly repeated them in an undertone, then, turning to Hero, gave the order in a clear, deep voice, that seemed to thrill the dog with its familiar ring. Instantly at the sound he started out across the field. Not a thing that had been taught him in his long, careful training was forgotten.

The first man he found was lying in a ditch, apparently desperately wounded. Hero allowed him to help himself from his flask, and drag a bandage from the bags on his back. Then, standing with his hind feet in the ditch and his fore feet resting on the bank above him, he gave voice until the men by the ambulance heard him, and came toward him carrying a stretcher.

"Look at him!" exclaimed Mrs. Walton, who with the party and several of the officers had walked down to the hospital tent. "He knows he has done his duty well. Did you ever see a dog manifest such delight! He fairly wriggles with joy!"

The praise of the men bearing the stretcher, and especially of the orderly, seemed to send the dog into a transport of happiness. The second man lay far on the outskirts of the field, hidden by a thicket of hazel bushes. This time Hero's frantic barking brought no reply. The men acted as if deaf to his appeals of help, so in a few minutes, evidently thinking they were beyond the range of his voice, he picked up the man's cap in his mouth, and ran back at the top of his speed.

"Good dog!" said the orderly, taking the cap he dropped at his feet. "Go back now and lead the way."

"If that man had really been wounded, and had crawled under that thicket," said Colonel Wayne, "we never could have found him alone. Only the sense of smell could lead to such a hiding-place. The ambulance might have passed there a hundred times and never seen a trace of him."

The hunt went on for some time; before it closed, every man personating a killed or wounded soldier was located and carried to the hospital tent. When the tired dog was finally allowed to rest, he dropped down at the orderly's feet, panting.

"That was certainly fine work," said the Colonel, stooping to pat Hero's sides. "I suppose nothing could induce you to give him up to the army?" he asked, turning to Lloyd.

"Oh, no, no, no!" cried Lloyd, as if alarmed at the suggestion, and pressing Hero's head protectingly against her shoulder. If she had been proud of him before, she was doubly proud of him now. He had won the admiration of the entire regiment. Never had he been so praised and petted. When Mrs. Walton called her party together for their homeward drive, it was plain to be seen that Hero was loath to leave the camp. A word from the orderly would have kept him, despite Lloyd's commands to jump up into the wagon.

As the boys rode on ahead again, Keith said, "It does seem too bad to force that dog into being a private citizen when he is a born soldier."

"Did you hear what Colonel Wayne told mamma as we left?" asked Ranald. "He told her that it was reported that some of the animals had escaped from the circus that was in Louisville yesterday, and that a panther and some other kind of a beast had been seen in these woods. He laughed and asked her if she didn't want him to send a guard over to our camp. Of course he was only joking, but when she saw that I had heard what he said, she told me not to tell the girls; not to even mention such a thing, or they'd be so frightened they'd want to break camp and go straight home."

"It would be fun to scare them," said Rob, "but you'd better believe I'll not say anything if there's any danger of having to go home sooner on account of it."

"We've got to go day after to-morrow anyhow," said Keith, gloomily. "I wish I could miss another week of school, but I know papa wouldn't let me, even if the camp didn't break up."

"Come on!" called Ranald, who had pushed on ahead. "Let's hurry back and have a good swim before supper."

Not satisfied with the excitement of the day, the girls were no sooner out of the wagon than some one started a wild game of prisoners' base. Then they played hide-and-seek among the rocks and trees around the waterfall, and while they were wiping their flushed faces, panting after the long run, Kitty proposed that they should have a candy pulling.

Dinah made the candy, but the girls pulled it, running a race to see whose would be the whitest in a given time. Their arms ached long before they were done. By the time the boys came stumbling up the hill from their long swim in the creek, it would be hard to say which group was most tired.

"I'm sure we'll all want to turn in early to-night,"
said Mrs. Walton at supper.   Freddy was yawning
widely, and Elise was almost asleep over her plate.
"You are all tired."

"All but Hero," said Miss Allison, offering him
a chicken bone.   "He rested while the others
played.   You'd like to go through your game every
day.   Wouldn't you, old boy?"

There was no story-telling around the camp-fire
that night.   They gathered around it, even before
the light died out in the sky.   Ranald had his guitar
and Allison her mandolin, and they thrummed ac-
companiments awhile for the others to sing.   But a
mighty yawn catching Margery in the middle of a
verse, and Mrs. Walton discovering both Jamie and
Freddy sound asleep on the rug beside her, she proposed that they all go to bed an hour earlier than
usual.

The Little Captain vowed he was too sleepy to
blow a single toot on his bugle, so they went to
their tents without the usual sounding of taps.   It
was not long before every child was asleep, worn
out by the day's hard play.   Mrs. Walton lay awake
sometime listening to the sounds outside the tent.
The crackling of underbrush and rustle of dry leaves
was familiar enough in the daytime, but they seemed

strangely ominous now that the lights were out. She could not help thinking of what the Colonel had told her of the escaped panther. She imagined the panic it would make if it should suddenly appear in their midst. Then she thought of Hero's protecting presence, and, raising herself on her elbow, she looked across the tent to where she knew he lay asleep. At first she could not see even the ruff of white that made the collar around his tawny throat, for the moon had slipped behind a cloud, but as she raised herself on her elbow, and peered intently through the darkness, the faint misty light shone out again, and she saw Hero plainly, the Little Colonel's outstretched hand resting on his broad back. Then she lay down again, this time to sleep, and soon all the little camp was wrapped in the peace and rest of perfect silence.

Half an hour later Hero lifted his head from between his paws and listened. Something seemed calling him. He did not know what. Being only a dog, he could not analyse the thoughts passing through his brain. A restlessness seized him. He longed to be back among the familiar sights and sounds of soldier life. This little play camp, where children tried to make him romp continually, was not home. Locust was not home. This strange new country full of unfamiliar faces and foreign voices was not home. But the orderly's voice reminded him of it. Over there were bearded men and deep voices, and strong hands, guns, and the smell of powder; fife and drum, and canteens and knapsacks; things that he had seen daily in his soldier life.

Was it some call to duty that thrilled him, or only a homesick longing? As he listened with head up, there came ringing, clear and silvery through the night, the bugle notes from the other camp. At the first sound Hero was on his feet. He moved noiselessly toward the tent flap, only partially fastened, and flattening himself against the ground wriggled out.

And if he gave no thought to the little mistress dreaming inside the tent, if he left without regret the life of ease and loving care to which she had brought him, it was not because he was ungrateful, but because he did not understand. To him his old life woke and called him in the bugle's blowing. To him duty did not mean soft cushions, and idle days, and the following of a happy-hearted child at play. It meant long marches and the guarding of ambulances and the rescue of the dead and dying. A true soldier's heart beat in the dog's shaggy body, and, obedient to his instinct and training, he answered the summons when it sounded. With long, swinging steps he set out in the direction of the bugle-call, taking the road through the woods that the wagon had travelled that day, and down which he had watched the orderly disappear. No, not deserting his duty, but, as he understood it, hurrying back with faithful heart to the cause that had always claimed him.

Now and then the moon, coming out fitfully from behind the clouds, shone on his great tawny body, touching the white curls of his ruff with a line of silver. Then he would be lost in darkness again. But he swung on unerringly, until he was almost in sight of the camp. A little farther on a sentry paced up and down the picket-line that ran along the edge of the woods. Hero travelled on toward him, the dry dead leaves rustling under his paws, and now and then a twig crackling with his weight.

The sentry paused and listened, wondering what kind of an animal was coming toward him in the darkness.

"Halt! Who goes there?" he called, sharply. The moon, peeping out at that instant, seemed to magnify the size of the great creature in his path. He thought of the panther and the other wild beast, whatever it was, supposed to be roaming about in the woods. Then the moon disappeared as suddenly as it had lighted up the scene, and the big paws still pattered on toward him in the darkness, regardless of his repeated challenge.

As the underbrush crackled again with the weight of the great body now almost upon him, the sentry raised his rifle. A shot rang out, arousing the camp not yet fully settled to sleep. The echo bounded back from the startled hills, and rolled away over the peaceful farms and orchards, growing fainter and fainter, until only a whisper of it reached the white tent where the Little Colonel lay dreaming. Then the moon shone out again, and the sentry, going a few paces forward, looked down in horror at the silent form stretched out at his feet.

CHAPTER XVI.

"TAPS"

THE corporal of the guard went running in the direction of the shot, and here and there an inquiring head was thrust out of a tent.

"Only a dog shot, sir," he was heard to call out in answer to some officer's question, as he passed back down the line. "Sentry took him for a wild beast escaped from the show."

Somebody laughed in reply, and the men who had been aroused by the noise turned over and went to sleep. They did not know that the corporal hurried on down to the guard-house, and that as a result of his report there was a hasty summons for the surgeon. They did not know that it was Hero whom the sentry bent over, gulping down a feeling in his throat that nearly choked him, as he saw the blood welling out of the dog's shaggy white breast, and slowly stiffening the silky hair of his beautiful yellow coat.

The surgeon knelt down beside the dog, and as

the clouds hid the moon again, he turned the light of his lantern on the wound for a careful examination.

"That was a cracking good shot, Bently," he said. "He never knew what stopped him."

The sentry turned his head away. "I wouldn't have been the one to take that dog's life for anything in the world!" he exclaimed. "I'd pretty near as soon have killed a man. It never entered my head that any tame animal would come leaping out of the woods that way at this time of night. He loomed up nearly as big as a lion when the moon shone out on him. The next minute it was all dark again, and I heard his big soft feet come pattering through the leaves, straight on toward me. It flashed over me that it must be one of those escaped circus animals, so I just let loose and blazed away at him."

The surgeon stood up and looked down at the still form at his feet. "It's too bad," he said. "He was a grand old dog, the finest St. Bernard I ever saw. How that little girl loved him! It will just about break her heart when she finds out what's happened to him."

"Don't!" begged the sentry, huskily. "Don't say anything like that. I feel bad enough about it now, goodness knows, without your harrowing up my feelings, talking of the way *she's* going to feel."

As the surgeon started on, the sentry stopped him. "For heaven's sake, Mac, don't leave him lying there on the picket-line where I've got to see him every time I pass. Send somebody to take him away. I'm all unnerved. I feel as if I'd shot one of my own comrades."

The surgeon looked at him curiously and walked on. Nobody was sent to take the dog away, but a little while later the sentry was relieved from duty, and another soldier kept guard over the silent camp, pacing back and forth past the Red Cross Hero, sleeping his last sleep under the light of the sentinel stars.

Somebody draped a flag across him before the camp was astir next morning. "Well, why not?" the man asked when he was joked about paying so much attention to a dead dog. "Why not? He was a war dog, wasn't he? It's no more than his due. I was the man he found in the ditch yesterday. As far as his intention and good will went, he did as much to save me as if I had been really lying there a wounded soldier. When he came leaping down there into the ditch after me, licking my face in such a friendly fashion and holding still so that I could help myself to the flask and bandages, I thought how grateful a fellow would feel to him if he were

really rescued by him that way. It was all make-
believe to me, but it was dead earnest to the dog,
and he did his part as faithfully as any soldier who
ever wore a uniform."

"You're right," said a young lieutenant, sitting
near. "If for no other reason than that he was in
the service of the Red Cross, he has a right to the
respect of every man that calls himself a soldier, no
matter what flag he follows."

Later in the morning, when the orderly rode into
the little picnic camp, the girls were away. They
were down by the waterfall digging ferns and mosses
to take home. "We are thinking of breaking up
camp this afternoon," Mrs. Walton told him. "The
weather looks so threatening that I have sent for the
wagonette to come for us, and I was about to send
over to your camp to see if Hero had wandered back
there. He has not been seen since last night. He
was lying by Lloyd's cot just before I went to sleep,
but this morning he is nowhere to be found. Lloyd
is distressed. I told her that probably the drill yesterday awakened all his love for the old life, and that
he might have been drawn back to it. Was I right?
Have you seen him?"

"Yes," said the orderly, hesitating. "I saw him,
but I find it hard to tell you how and where, Mrs.

Walton." He paused again, and then hurried on with the explanation, as if anxious to have it over as soon as possible.

"He was shot last night by mistake on the picket-line. The sentry is all broken up over it, poor fellow, and the whole camp regrets it more than I can tell. You see, after yesterday's performance we almost claimed the dog as one of us. Colonel Wayne has made me the bearer of his deepest regrets. He especially deplores the occurrence on account of the dog's little mistress, knowing what a great grief it will be to her. He wishes, if you think it will be any consolation to her, to give Hero a military funeral, and bury him with the honours due a brave soldier."

"I am sure that Lloyd will want that," said Mrs. Walton. "She will appreciate it deeply, when she understands what a mark of respect to Hero such an attention would be. Tell Colonel Wayne, please, that I gladly accept the offer in her behalf, and will send Ranald over later, to arrange for it."

The orderly rode away, and Mrs. Walton turned to her sister, exclaiming, "Poor little Lloyd! I confess I am not brave enough to face her grief when she first hears the news. You will have to tell her, Allison. You know her so much better than I.

We might as well hurry the preparations for leaving. No one will care to stay a moment longer, now this has happened. It will cast a gloom over the entire party."

"Maybe it would be better not to tell her until after she gets home," suggested Miss Allison. She had soothed the childish griefs of nearly every child in the Valley, at some time or another, but she felt that this was the most serious one that had fallen to her lot to comfort.

"I'm sure it would be impossible to get Lloyd away from here without Hero, unless she knew," was the answer. "I heard her tell Kitty this morning that nobody could make her go without him. She said if he wasn't back by the time we were ready to start, we could go on without her, and she would hunt for him if it took all fall."

While they were still discussing it the boys came running back to camp much excited. They had met the orderly.

"Oh, the poor dog!" mourned Keith. "What a shame for the poor old fellow to be shot down that way. It seems almost as bad as if it had been one of us boys that was killed."

Ranald and Rob joined in with praise of his many lovable traits, talking of his death as if it were a lifelong friend they had lost ; but Malcolm turned away with an anxious glance to the woods, where he could hear the laughing voices of the girls.

"Poor little Princess Winsome," he thought. "It will nearly break her heart," and he wished with all the earnestness of the real Sir Feal, that by some knightly service, no matter how hard, he could save his little friend from this sorrow.

The girls came strolling up, presently, so occupied with their spoils that no one noticed the boys' serious faces but Lloyd. The moment she caught Malcolm's sympathetic glance she was sure something had happened to Hero.

"Oh, what is it ?" she began, the tears gathering in her eyes as she felt the unspoken sympathy of the little group. Leaving Mrs. Walton to tell the other girls, Miss Allison drew Lloyd aside, saying as she led her down toward the spring, an arm around her waist, "I have a message for you, Lloyd, from Colonel Wayne. Let's go down to the rocks by ourselves."

A sympathetic silence fell on the little circle left behind as they heard Lloyd cry out, "Shot my dog ? Shot *Hero ?* Oh, he ought to be killed! How could he do such a cruel thing!"

"But he feels dreadfully about it," said Miss Allison. "The orderly said that, big, strong man though he was, the tears stood in his eyes when he saw what he had done, and he kept saying, 'I wouldn't have done it for the world.'"

Nearly all the girls were crying by this time, and Malcolm turned his head so that he could not see the fair little head pressed against Miss Allison's shoulder, as she clung to her sobbing.

"Think how it must have hurt poah Hero's feelin's," Lloyd was saying, "to go back to their camp so trustin' and happy, thinkin' the men would be so glad to see him, and that he was doin' his duty, and then to have one of them stand up and send a bullet through his deah, lovin' old heart. Oh, I can't *beah* it," she screamed. "Oh, I can't! I can't! It seems as if it would kill me to think of him lyin' ovah there all cold and stiff, with the blood on his lovely white and yellow curls, and know that he'll nevah, nevah again jump up to lick my hands, and put his paws on my shouldahs. He'll nevah come to meet me any moah, waggin' his tail and lookin' up into my face with his deah lovin' eyes. Oh, Miss Allison! I can't stand it! It's just breakin' my heart!" Burying her face in Miss Allison's lap, she sobbed and cried until her tears were all spent.

It was a subdued little party that rode back to the

Valley, a few hours later. Not only sympathy for Lloyd kept them quiet, but each one mourned the loss of the gentle, lovable playfellow who had come to such an untimely end after this week of happy camp life with them.

Under the locusts that evening, just as the sun was going down, came the tread of many marching feet. It was the tramp, tramp of the soldiers who were bringing home the Little Colonel's Hero. All the men who had been most interested in his performances the day before, had volunteered to follow Colonel Wayne, and the long line made an imposing showing, as it stretched up the avenue after him.

Lloyd watched the approach from her seat on the porch beside her father. All the camping party were waiting with her, except the four boys who rode at the head of the procession. Ranald and Malcolm first, then Rob and Keith. Lloyd hid her eyes as Lad and Tarbaby came into view behind them.

"Look," said her father gently, pointing to the flag-draped burden they drew. "How much better it was for Hero to have been shot by a soldier and brought home with military honours, than to have met the fate of an ordinary dog — been poisoned, or mangled by a train, as might have happened, or

even died of a painful, feeble old age. The Major
would have chosen this ; so would Hero, if he could
have understood."

There was more comfort in that thought than in
anything that had been said to her before, and Lloyd
wiped her eyes, and sat up to watch the ceremony
that followed, with a feeling of pride that made her
almost cheerful.

On they came to the beat of the muffled drum,
halting under a great locust-tree that stood by itself
on the lawn, in sight of the library windows, like
a giant sentinel. There the boys dismounted to
lower Hero into the grave that Walker and Alec had
just finished digging. Then the coloured men, spread-
ing the sod quickly back in place, stepped aside from
the low mound they had made, and Lloyd saw that it
was smooth and green. She started violently when
the soldiers, drawn up in line, fired a parting volley
over it, but sat quietly back again when the Little
Captain stepped forward and raised his bugle. The
sun was sinking low behind the locusts, and in the
golden glow filling the western sky, he softly sounded
taps. " Lights out " now for the faithful old Hero !
The last bugle-call that sounded for him was in
a foreign land, but it was not as a stranger and
an alien they left him.

The flag he followed floats farther than the Stars and Stripes, waves wider than the banner of the Kaiser. It is a world-wide flag, that flag of perpetual peace which bears the Red Cross of Geneva. In its shadow, whether on land or sea, all patriot hearts are at home, and under that flag they left him.

A square white stone stands now under the locust where the Little Captain sounded taps at the close of that September day. On it gleams the Red Cross, in whose service all of Hero's lessons had been learned. But the daily sight of it from her bedroom window no longer brings pain to the Little Colonel. Hero is only a tender memory now, and she counts the Red Cross above him as another talisman, like the little ring and the silver scissors, to remind her that only through unselfish service to others can one reach the happiness that is highest and best.

Time flies fast under the locusts. Sometimes to Papa Jack it seems only yesterday that she clattered up and down the wide halls with her grandfather's spurs buckled to her tiny feet. But if he misses the charm of the baby voice that called to him then, or the childish mischievousness of his Little Colonel, he finds a greater one in the flower-like beauty of the tall, slender girl who stands beside the gilded

harp, and sings to him softly in the candle-light.
And it is Betty's song of service that is oftenest on
her lips :

> " My godmother bids me spin,
> That my heart may not be sad;
> Sing and spin for my brother's sake,
> And the spinning makes me glad."

She knows that she can never be a Joan of Arc
or a Clara Barton, and her name will never be written
in America's hall of fame, but with the sweet am-
bition in her heart to make life a little lovelier for
every one she touches, she is growing up into a
veritable Princess Winsome.

Often as she sings, Betty closes her book to listen,
thrilled with the old feeling that always comes with
the music of the harp. It is as if she were "away
off from everything, and high up where it is
wide and open, and where the stars are." The
strange, beautiful thoughts she can find no words
for still dance on ahead, like shining will-'o-the-
wisps, but she knows that she shall surely find
words for them some day, and that many besides the
Little Colonel will sing her verses and find comfort
in her songs.

To both Betty and Lloyd the land of Someday
and the happy land of Now lie very close together

in their day-dreams, as side by side they go to school these bright October mornings, or stroll slowly homeward in the golden afternoons, under the shade of the friendly old locusts.

THE END.

Selections from The Page Company's Books for Young People

THE BLUE BONNET SERIES

Each large 12mo, cloth decorative, illustrated,
per volume **$1.50**

A TEXAS BLUE BONNET
By Caroline E. Jacobs.

"The book's heroine, Blue Bonnet, has the very finest kind of wholesome, honest, lively girlishness."—*Chicago Inter-Ocean.*

BLUE BONNET'S RANCH PARTY
By Caroline E. Jacobs and Edyth Ellerbeck Read.

"A healthy, natural atmosphere breathes from every chapter."—*Boston Transcript.*

BLUE BONNET IN BOSTON; Or, Boarding-School Days at Miss North's.
By Caroline E. Jacobs and Lela Horn Richards.

"It is bound to become popular because of its wholesomeness and its many human touches."—*Boston Globe.*

BLUE BONNET KEEPS HOUSE; Or, The New Home in the East.
By Caroline E. Jacobs and Lela Horn Richards.

"It cannot fail to prove fascinating to girls in their teens."—*New York Sun.*

BLUE BONNET—DÉBUTANTE
By Lela Horn Richards.

An interesting picture of the unfolding of life for Blue Bonnet.

A—1

THE YOUNG PIONEER SERIES

By Harrison Adams

Each 12mo, cloth decorative, illustrated, per volume **$1.25**

THE PIONEER BOYS OF THE OHIO; Or, Clearing the Wilderness.

" Such books as this are an admirable means of stimulating among the young Americans of to-day interest in the story of their pioneer ancestors and the early days of the Republic." — *Boston Globe.*

THE PIONEER BOYS ON THE GREAT LAKES; Or, On the Trail of the Iroquois.

" The recital of the daring deeds of the frontier is not only interesting but instructive as well and shows the sterling type of character which these days of self-reliance and trial produced." — *American Tourist, Chicago.*

THE PIONEER BOYS OF THE MISSISSIPPI; Or, The Homestead in the Wilderness.

" The story is told with spirit, and is full of adventure."—*New York Sun.*

THE PIONEER BOYS OF THE MISSOURI; Or, In the Country of the Sioux.

" Vivid in style, vigorous in movement, full of dramatic situations, true to historic perspective, this story is a capital one for boys."—*Watchman Examiner, New York City.*

THE PIONEER BOYS OF THE YELLOW- STONE; Or, Lost in the Land of Wonders.

" There is plenty of lively adventure and action and the story is well told."—*Duluth Herald, Duluth, Minn.*

THE PIONEER BOYS OF THE COLUMBIA; Or, In the Wilderness of the Great Northwest.

" The story is full of spirited action and contains much valuable historical information."—*Boston Herald.*

A—2

THE HADLEY HALL SERIES
By Louise M. Breitenbach

Each large 12mo, cloth decorative, illustrated, per volume **$1.50**

ALMA AT HADLEY HALL
" The author is to be congratulated on having written such an appealing book for girls." — *Detroit Free Press.*

ALMA'S SOPHOMORE YEAR
" It cannot fail to appeal to the lovers of good things in girls' books." — *Boston Herald.*

ALMA'S JUNIOR YEAR
" The diverse characters in the boarding-school are strongly drawn, the incidents are well developed and the action is never dull." — *The Boston Herald.*

ALMA'S SENIOR YEAR
" Incident abounds in all of Miss Breitenbach's stories and a healthy, natural atmosphere breathes from every chapter." — *Boston Transcript.*

THE GIRLS OF FRIENDLY TERRACE SERIES
By Harriet Lummis Smith

Each large 12mo, cloth decorative, illustrated, per volume **$1.50**

THE GIRLS OF FRIENDLY TERRACE
" A book sure to please girl readers, for the author seems to understand perfectly the girl character." — *Boston Globe.*

PEGGY RAYMOND'S VACATION
" It is a wholesome, hearty story."—*Utica Observer.*

PEGGY RAYMOND'S SCHOOL DAYS
The book is delightfully written, and contains lots of exciting incidents.

A—3

FAMOUS LEADERS SERIES

By Charles H. L. Johnston

Each large 12mo, cloth decorative, illustrated, per volume **$1.50**

FAMOUS CAVALRY LEADERS

" More of such books should be written, books that acquaint young readers with historical personages in a pleasant, informal way." — *New York Sun.*

" It is a book that will stir the heart of every boy and will prove interesting as well to the adults." — *Lawrence Daily World.*

FAMOUS INDIAN CHIEFS

" Mr. Johnston has done faithful work in this volume, and his relation of battles, sieges and struggles of these famous Indians with the whites for the possession of America is a worthy addition to United States History." — *New York Marine Journal.*

FAMOUS SCOUTS

" It is the kind of a book that will have a great fascination for boys and young men, and while it entertains them it will also present valuable information in regard to those who have left their impress upon the history of the country." — *The New London Day.*

FAMOUS PRIVATEERSMEN AND ADVENTURERS OF THE SEA

" The tales are more than merely interesting; they are entrancing, stirring the blood with thrilling force and bringing new zest to the never-ending interest in the dramas of the sea." — *The Pittsburgh Post.*

FAMOUS FRONTIERSMEN AND HEROES OF THE BORDER

" The accounts are not only authentic, but distinctly readable, making a book of wide appeal to all who love the history of actual adventure." — *Cleveland Leader.*

FAMOUS DISCOVERERS AND EXPLORERS OF AMERICA

" The book is an epitome of some of the wildest and bravest adventures of which the world has known and of discoveries which have changed the face of the old world as well as of the new." — *Brooklyn Daily Eagle.*

A—4

HILDEGARDE-MARGARET SERIES

By Laura E. Richards

Eleven Volumes

The Hildegarde-Margaret Series, beginning with "Queen Hildegarde" and ending with "The Merryweathers," make one of the best and most popular series of books for girls ever written.

Each large 12mo, cloth decorative, illustrated,
per volume $1.35
The eleven volumes boxed as a set . . . $14.85

LIST OF TITLES

QUEEN HILDEGARDE

HILDEGARDE'S HOLIDAY

HILDEGARDE'S HOME

HILDEGARDE'S NEIGHBORS

HILDEGARDE'S HARVEST

THREE MARGARETS

MARGARET MONTFORT

PEGGY

RITA

FERNLEY HOUSE

THE MERRYWEATHERS
A—5

THE CAPTAIN JANUARY SERIES

By Laura E. Richards

Each one volume, 12mo, cloth decorative, illustrated, per volume 60 cents

CAPTAIN JANUARY

A charming idyl of New England coast life, whose success has been very remarkable.

SAME. *Illustrated Holiday Edition* . . $1.35

MELODY: The Story of a Child.

MARIE

A companion to "Melody" and "Captain January."

ROSIN THE BEAU

A sequel to "Melody" and "Marie."

SNOW-WHITE; Or, The House in the Wood.

JIM OF HELLAS; Or, In Durance Vile, and a companion story, Bethesda Pool.

NARCISSA

And a companion story, In Verona, being two delightful short stories of New England life.

"SOME SAY"

And a companion story, Neighbors in Cyrus.

NAUTILUS

"'Nautilus' is by far the best product of the author's powers, and is certain to achieve the wide success it so richly merits."

ISLA HERON

This interesting story is written in the author's usual charming manner.

THE LITTLE MASTER

"A well told, interesting tale of a high character." — *California Gateway Gazette.*

A—6

DELIGHTFUL BOOKS FOR LITTLE FOLKS

By Laura E. Richards

THREE MINUTE STORIES

Cloth decorative, 12mo, with eight plates in full color and many text illustrations .   .   . $1.35
"Little ones will understand and delight in the stories and poems." — *Indianapolis News.*

FIVE MINUTE STORIES

Cloth decorative, square 12mo, illustrated . $1.35
A charming collection of short stories and clever poems for children.

MORE FIVE MINUTE STORIES

Cloth decorative, square 12mo, illustrated . $1.35
A noteworthy collection of short stories and poems for children, which will prove as popular with mothers as with boys and girls.

FIVE MICE IN A MOUSE TRAP

Cloth decorative, square 12mo, illustrated . $1.35
The story of their lives and other wonderful things related by the Man in the Moon, done in the vernacular from the lunacular form by Laura E. Richards.

POLLYANNA ANNUAL NO. 1

Trade Mark
The Yearly GLAD Book.
Trade ———— Mark
Edited by Florence Orville.
Large octavo, with nearly 200 illustrations, 12 in full color, bound with an all-over pictorial cover design in colors, with fancy printed end papers. $1.50

"The contents of this splendid volume are evidently intended to demonstrate the fact that work is as good a glad game as play if gone about the right way. There are clever little drawings any one could imitate, and in imitating learn something. There are adventurous tales, fairy tales, scientific tales, comic stories and serious stories in verse and prose." — *Montreal Herald and Star.*

A—7

THE BOYS' STORY OF THE RAILROAD SERIES

By Burton E. Stevenson

Each large 12mo, cloth decorative, illustrated, per volume $1.50

THE YOUNG SECTION-HAND; Or, The Adventures of Allan West.

"The whole range of section railroading is covered in the story." — *Chicago Post.*

THE YOUNG TRAIN DISPATCHER

"A vivacious account of the varied and often hazardous nature of railroad life." — *Congregationalist.*

THE YOUNG TRAIN MASTER

"It is a book that can be unreservedly commended to anyone who loves a good, wholesome, thrilling, informing yarn." — *Passaic News.*

THE YOUNG APPRENTICE; Or, Allan West's Chum.

"The story is intensely interesting." — *Baltimore Sun.*

STORIES BY BREWER CORCORAN

Each, one volume, 12mo, cloth decorative, illustrated, per volume $1.50

THE BOY SCOUTS OF KENDALLVILLE

Published with the approval of "The Boy Scouts of America."

The story of a bright young factory worker who cannot enlist because he has three dependents, but his knowledge of woodcraft and wig-wagging gained through Scout practice enables him to foil a German plot to blow up the munitions factory.

THE BARBARIAN; Or, Will Bradford's School Days at St. Jo's.

"This is a splendid story of friendship, study and sport, winding up with a perfectly corking double play." — *Springfield Union.*

A—8

THE LITTLE COLONEL BOOKS
(Trade Mark)

By ANNIE FELLOWS JOHNSTON

Each large 12mo, cloth, illustrated, per volume . $1.50

THE LITTLE COLONEL STORIES
(Trade Mark)

Being three " Little Colonel " stories in the Cosy Corner Series, " The Little Colonel," " Two Little Knights of Kentucky," and " The Giant Scissors," in a single volume.

THE LITTLE COLONEL'S HOUSE PARTY
(Trade Mark)

THE LITTLE COLONEL'S HOLIDAYS
(Trade Mark)

THE LITTLE COLONEL'S HERO
(Trade Mark)

THE LITTLE COLONEL AT BOARDING-
(Trade Mark)
SCHOOL

THE LITTLE COLONEL IN ARIZONA
(Trade Mark)

THE LITTLE COLONEL'S CHRISTMAS
(Trade Mark)
VACATION

THE LITTLE COLONEL, MAID OF HONOR
(Trade Mark)

THE LITTLE COLONEL'S KNIGHT COMES
(Trade Mark)
RIDING

THE LITTLE COLONEL'S CHUM, MARY
WARE (Trade Mark)

MARY WARE IN TEXAS

MARY WARE'S PROMISED LAND

These twelve volumes, boxed as a set, $18.00.

A—9

SPECIAL HOLIDAY EDITIONS

Each small quarto, cloth decorative, per volume . $1.35

New plates, handsomely illustrated with eight full-page drawings in color, and many marginal sketches.

THE LITTLE COLONEL
(Trade Mark)
TWO LITTLE KNIGHTS OF KENTUCKY
THE GIANT SCISSORS
BIG BROTHER

THE JOHNSTON JEWEL SERIES

Each small 16mo, cloth decorative, with frontispiece and decorative text borders, per volume $0.60

IN THE DESERT OF WAITING: The Legend of Camelback Mountain.

THE THREE WEAVERS: A Fairy Tale for Fathers and Mothers as Well as for Their Daughters.

KEEPING TRYST: A Tale of King Arthur's Time.

THE LEGEND OF THE BLEEDING HEART

THE RESCUE OF PRINCESS WINSOME: A Fairy Play for Old and Young.

THE JESTER'S SWORD

THE LITTLE COLONEL'S GOOD TIMES BOOK

Uniform in size with the Little Colonel Series . $1.50

Bound in white kid (morocco) and gold . 3.00

Cover design and decorations by Peter Verberg.

" A mighty attractive volume in which the owner may record the good times she has on decorated pages, and under the directions as it were of Annie Fellows Johnston." — *Buffalo Express.*

A—10

THE LITTLE COLONEL DOLL BOOK —
First Series
Quarto, boards, printed in colors . . . $1.50
A series of "Little Colonel" dolls. Each has several changes of costume, so they can be appropriately clad for the rehearsal of any scene or incident in the series.

THE LITTLE COLONEL DOLL BOOK—
Second Series
Quarto, boards, printed in colors . . . $1.50
An artistic series of paper dolls, including not only lovable Mary Ware, the Little Colonel's chum, but many another of the much loved characters which appear in the last three volumes of the famous "Little Colonel Series."

ASA HOLMES
By ANNIE FELLOWS JOHNSTON.
With a frontispiece by Ernest Fosbery.
16mo, cloth decorative, gilt top . . . $1.00
"'Asa Holmes' is the most delightful, most sympathetic and wholesome book that has been published in a long while." — *Boston Times.*

TRAVELERS FIVE: ALONG LIFE'S HIGHWAY
By ANNIE FELLOWS JOHNSTON.
With an introduction by Bliss Carman, and a frontispiece by E. H. Garrett.
12mo, cloth decorative $1.25
"Mrs. Johnston broadens her reputation with this book so rich in the significance of common things." — *Boston Advertiser.*

JOEL: A BOY OF GALILEE
By ANNIE FELLOWS JOHNSTON.
12mo, cloth decorative, illustrated . . . $1.50
"The book is a very clever handling of the greatest event in the history of the world." — *Rochester, N. Y., Herald.*

A—11

THE BOYS' STORY OF THE ARMY SERIES

By Florence Kimball Russel

BORN TO THE BLUE

12mo, cloth decorative, illustrated . . . $1.50
"The story deserves warm commendation and genuine popularity."—*Army and Navy Register.*

IN WEST POINT GRAY

12mo, cloth decorative, illustrated . . . $1.50
"One of the best books that deals with West Point."—*New York Sun.*

FROM CHEVRONS TO SHOULDER-STRAPS

12mo, cloth decorative, illustrated . . . $1.50
"The life of a cadet at West Point is portrayed very realistically."—*The Hartford Post, Hartford, Conn.*

DOCTOR'S LITTLE GIRL SERIES

By Marion Ames Taggart
Each large 12mo, cloth, illustrated, per volume, **$1.50**

THE DOCTOR'S LITTLE GIRL

"A charming story of the ups and downs of the life of a dear little maid."—*The Churchman.*

SWEET NANCY: The Further Adventures of the Doctor's Little Girl.

"Just the sort of book to amuse, while its influence cannot but be elevating."—*New York Sun.*

NANCY, THE DOCTOR'S LITTLE PARTNER

"The story is sweet and fascinating, such as many girls of wholesome tastes will enjoy."—*Springfield Union.*

NANCY PORTER'S OPPORTUNITY

"Nancy shows throughout that she is a splendid young woman, with plenty of pluck."—*Boston Globe.*

NANCY AND THE COGGS TWINS

"The story is refreshing."—*New York Sun.*

A—12

WORKS OF EVALEEN STEIN

THE CHRISTMAS PORRINGER

12mo, cloth decorative, illustrated by Adelaide
Everhart **$1.25**
This story happened many hundreds of years ago in
the quaint Flemish city of Bruges and concerns a little
girl named Karen, who worked at lace-making with her
aged grandmother.

GABRIEL AND THE HOUR BOOK

Small quarto, cloth decorative, illustrated and
decorated in colors by Adelaide Everhart . . $1.25
" No works in juvenile fiction contain so many of the
elements that stir the hearts of children and grown-ups as
well as do the stories so admirably told by this author."
— *Louisville Daily Courier.*

A LITTLE SHEPHERD OF PROVENCE

12mo, cloth decorative, illustrated by Diantha
H. Marlowe $1.25
" The story should be one of the influences in the life
of every child to whom good stories can be made to
appeal." — *Public Ledger.*

THE LITTLE COUNT OF NORMANDY

12mo, cloth decorative, illustrated by John Goss $1.25
" This touching and pleasing story is told with a wealth
of interest coupled with enlivening descriptions of the
country where its scenes are laid and of the people thereof."
— *Wilmington Every Evening.*

THE HOUSE ON THE HILL

By MARGARET R. PIPER, author of " Sylvia Arden,"
" Sylvia of the Hill Top," " Sylvia Arden Decides," etc.
12mo, cloth decorative, illustrated . . . $1.50
" It is a bright, entertaining story, with happy young
folks, good times, natural development, and a gentle
earnestness of general tone." — *The Christian Register,
Boston.*

A—13

HISTORICAL BOOKS

THE BOYS OF '61; Or, Four Years of Fighting.
By Charles Carleton Coffin.

Extra Illustrated Edition. An entirely new edition, cloth decorative, 8vo, with nearly two hundred illustrations $2.00

Regular Edition. Cloth decorative, 12mo, with eight illustrations $1.35

A record of personal observation with the Army and Navy, from the Battle of Bull Run to the fall of Richmond.

THE BOYS OF 1812; And Other Naval Heroes.
By James Russell Soley.

Cloth, 8vo, illustrated $2.00

"The book is full of stirring incidents and adventures." — *Boston Herald.*

THE SAILOR BOYS OF '61
By James Russell Soley.

Cloth, 8vo, illustrated $2.00

"It is written with an enthusiasm that never allows the interest to slacken."—*The Call, Newark, N. J.*

BOYS OF FORT SCHUYLER
By James Otis.

Cloth decorative, square 12mo, illustrated . $1.25

"It is unquestionably one of the best historical Indian stories ever written."—*Boston Herald.*

FAMOUS WAR STORIES
By Charles Carleton Coffin

Each cloth decorative, 12mo, illustrated, per vol., $1.25

WINNING HIS WAY
A story of a young soldier in the Civil War.

MY DAYS AND NIGHTS ON THE BATTLEFIELD
A story of the Battle of Bull Run and other battles in Kentucky, Tennessee, and on the Mississippi.

FOLLOWING THE FLAG
A story of the Army of the Potomac in the Civil War.

A—14